TOPICALITY
Modern Themes for Modern Times

Topicality
Modern Themes for Modern Times

Christophe Little

JANUS PUBLISHING COMPANY
London, England

First Published in Great Britain 2007
by Janus Publishing Company Ltd,
105-107 Gloucester Place,
London W1U 6BY

www.januspublishing.co.uk

British Library Cataloguing-in-Publication Data
A catalogue record for this book
is available from the British Library

ISBN 978-1-85756-647-5

Cover Design: Janus Publishing

Cover photograph by John Hall.
www.ConcordePhotographs.com

Printed and bound in Great Britain

This book is dedicated to my Mother.

Contents

Preface

Topicality simply gave me the excuse to write about anything that tickled my interest. It has to be said right from the start that this book contains no central plot or theme but rather twenty different themes that, I'm sure, will engage anyone with an eye for the unconventional. The contents of Topicality derive almost entirely from my own personal experiences, which, I like to think, are varied enough to substantiate the themes touched on and, if I were to describe this book, I would call it a book of general interest fused together under a philosophical/theological lens. I have kept it short, not wishing to overindulge in my own reflections, while hoping to entertain the reader in the most detached style possible. To a certain extent, this work was driven by the drama of thought that pushes one to question one's existence, and it is with this in mind that Topicality should be looked upon.

1

Things American

The Land of Can Do lies approximately 3,000 miles in a westerly direction off Cabo da Roca, the western-most tip of the Iberian Peninsula, in Portugal. The Land of Can Do is known for being big – very big. It has a surface area of 3,615,122 square miles and is divided into fifty separate territories. Have you guessed it yet? Yes, the Land of Can Do is none other than the United States of America.* What other fictional title could be given to this mammoth of a country that has the capacity to dwarf all other individual nations in terms of economy, wealth, power and military might? Thus, the Land of Can Do is a place where things can, and will, be done – or so I've been led to believe. To think of the States is to do so with a head full of preconceived ideas that one has difficulty getting rid of, considering the amount of media coverage it has received over the centuries. By writing this chapter without setting foot there, I am trying to rid myself of all those predisposed judgements that have no doubt affected my perception of the States. Indeed, this is an exercise in objectivity. Therefore, the following is a list of things that I have already heard, seen or read about the land talked about so often on TV.

In some ways, the United States has already formed my youth with programmes such as *Knight Rider*, *The A-Team*, *Street Hawk* and *Airwolf* not forgetting the likes of *Columbo*, *Starsky and Hutch* and *Miami Vice*, which, as with so many other series, make me feel as though I know the States already. Having grown up in an era of what I call high-quality TV programmes, my memories abound with thoughts of American

---

* The Land of Can Do gets its name from an article in the August 1994 edition of the *National Geographic* and features a group of students from South Carolina launching their own payload on the space shuttle *Endeavor*. Their project was named 'CAN DO' and I thought this phrase adequately captured the spirit of their nation.

cities vibrant with action and adventure, coloured with the most extraordinary larger than life characters that would prove to be fantastic subject material for any budding writer. Indeed, was it out of the alternate imagination of a surrealist writer that we heard the story of the man from New York who packaged himself in a cargo box to be posted to arrive at the front door of his parents' house in Dallas? It would certainly seem so. Or the story of the man, also from New York, who was taken to hospital after having been mauled by a Bengal tiger who just so happened to be his own pet, living in an apartment block alongside a three-foot alligator who had never seen the light of day? No, these were true-life events that make one understand the meaning of the phrase 'only in America'. Only in America could one witness pillagers during the 1992 Los Angeles Race Riots walk down the street carrying enormous three piece suites, and only in America could one watch live on network television O.J. Simpson being chased for arraignment by an array of police cars on the motorway cheered on by the shouts of onlookers, who chanted 'Go O.J.! Go O.J.!'

At this, the term 'weird and wonderful' comes to mind, or at least the term 'weird' does anyway. I say this in light of an unfortunate incident I experienced while attending a church service one Sunday in England. At the back of the church was a full bucket of holy water which was picked up and thrown over my head by a strange man who had previously told me that, on having visited the States, he found that there were many 'weirdos out there'. What was I to make from such a man's comment? If he noticed it, how was a supposedly 'normal' person to perceive the state of affairs? For some reason, it is hard not to imagine many such characters living over there.

Apart from these, I get the impression that America attracts those who aspire to wealth, fortune and power. Historically speaking, people have always flocked westwards in the hope of achieving their life-long ambition of settling in a country that would favour their material comfort and freedom. Today even, British actors, singers and entrepreneurs look to the west as a means of expanding their already-gained celebrity status. Those in show business are seeking confidently to follow in the footsteps of Charlie Chaplin, the world's first superstar, who, undoubtedly, was one of Britain's most famous exports to the States, while people like Richard Branson have thrived on the States' eagerness to offer his company a second home, making him one of the most successful businessmen ever to venture out across the Atlantic.

Need one be told of the number of celebrities in England who went in search of making it 'big' in America? They range from Catherine Zeta Jones to Gwyneth Paltrow, from Anthony Hopkins to Hugh Grant. It would appear that the confines of England are too small for their talent and that the much larger ones of the United States provide a natural springboard to propel them to superstardom.

It does not stop there. Other actors, such as Antonio Banderas from Spain, Pierce Brosnan from Ireland and Arnold Schwarzenegger from Austria, have all contributed to the hotch-potch of varying background nationalities that make up the modern-day superstate. The third person is a particular example in question. Having won the Mr Universe contest seven times, he then went on to appear in Hollywood blockbuster films that are all too typical of the 1980s and 1990s. His acquired fame enabled him to run for the post of governor of California in 2003 and win. It would seem that Arnold was born for America. One can hardly believe the similarities between the old muscle-man and Ronald Reagan, who also used the combination of acting and politics to catapult him to the fore. The only difference is that Schwarzenegger is destined never to become president due to his having been born in a foreign country. Yet, what does this tell us about *The Running Man?* He is not afraid of moving the levers of power. As a result of being physically more powerful than most, he moved from playing the roles of protagonists who in some way had an edge over others, to being given the role of most powerful man in California, the world's fifth largest economy. Arnold seems to be the very embodiment of the American success story.

All this could not have been attained without the necessary ingredient of confidence. I often find, when talking to an American citizen, that he or she oozes confidence to such a degree that the average Englishman may sometimes be intimidated by so radical a capacity to believe firmly in oneself. In America, one has to believe that success will be achieved through the driving force of one's own volition. A person over there instinctively knows that anything short of success will be an invitation for others to brand him or her 'a loser', hence, the race to become a 'winner'. Still, the high levels of American confidence could come from the fact that their country is number one in the world. They believe that theirs is the task of overcoming problems with the resource of human resilience and endurance. Nothing is to be feared. Jules Verne, in his book, *From Earth to the Moon*, commented on this following President Barbicane's communication to send a projectile to the lunar body:

> Nothing can astound an American. In America, all is easy, all is simple; and as for mechanical difficulties, they are overcome before they arise. Between Barbicane's proposition and its realisation no true Yankee would have allowed even the semblance of a difficulty to be possible. A thing with them is no sooner said than done.

In 1969, the French author's vision of America seeing through the first human exploration of the moon had been proved right. It is possibly only a matter of time before the same nation is responsible for the first human landing on Mars.

On a more terrestrial level, I know that race relations in the Land of Can Do are still an issue, bearing in mind the aforementioned Race Riots that took place in Los Angeles after too many black people thought it unfair for an all-white jury to have acquitted four police officers of the same colour who had been caught on camera beating to a pulp a black motorist by the name of Rodney King. I also know that from 1861 to 1865, a civil war broke out with the agenda of determining the predicament of black slaves in America. Luckily, those in favour of freeing the black population won, thus ensuring that all living under the constitution be treated fairly in accordance with equality. However, it still took someone like Martin Luther King to fight for the true civil rights of his own black countrymen. He was assassinated in Memphis.

Gun crime in America is rife. It is unfortunate that in Britain, we seem to be going down the same road. Across the Atlantic, the shocking news of some lunatic going on the rampage in a built-up area has all too often been synonymous with the storyline of a new Hollywood release. Who can forget the horrendous scene of two young students entering their college campus on a killing spree at Columbine High School in the late 1990s? The inhabitants of America, it would appear, have a strong reliance on the gun to solve their problems. It would be wise for one to avoid dark alleyways and back streets in a city like New York or Chicago; in the former, it was reported that Bob Warman, the Central News anchorman for the West Midlands, was mugged an amazing five times in one day. While composing this chapter, I was astounded to watch on the ITV News the absolutely unbelievable sight of two men in LA playing a game of hide and seek behind a tree outside some lawcourts. One of them had a pistol and was shooting at a desperately afraid lawyer, who took cover behind a tree trunk. It must be stated that the man with the gun was mere centimetres away from his proposed victim, yet he somehow managed repeatedly to miss his target, who dodged all the bullets but one (don't worry, he survived). This was made even more ludicrous by the fact that all this happened only metres away from a rolling camera that was there on an unrelated case. The man with the gun, on having no more ammunition, casually walked away as though going for a stroll in the park, seemingly impervious to his moment of madness. He was then rugby tackled by a security guard. Crazy? Certainly.

On a somewhat larger scale, September 11th, 2001, is one of those dates that send a shiver down the spine of any person imbued with the faculty of reason. It is one of those dates where everyone knows exactly what they were doing worldwide at 9 a.m. New York time, on that particular day. It is with a special tact that one must be made fully aware that Ground Zero was a huge gaping wound that deeply affected the American psyche. September 11th, from an alarmist's point of view, would change the outcome of the twenty-first century in the same way the First World War did the last. An optimist would argue that, despite severely undermining world peace, it does not change the day to day existence of the main body of the world's inhabitants. Whatever the opinion, I do believe that the date in question has brought forth the cancer of our epoch, plunging our fragile world into an alarming state of insecurity. If that sounds negative, one has to be reminded that we each have formed a judgement on the terrorist attacks in much the same vein as we have the release of the atomic bombs on Hiroshima and Nagasaki. September 11th is just too important to forget. The consequential wars in Afganistan and Iraq would confirm the need of President George W. Bush and Tony Blair to counter-balance the insecurity referred to. England and America, by standing shoulder to shoulder, have shared a moment in history that has pushed their 'special relationship' to its most intimate bond yet, notwithstanding the deep controversy caused by the war in Iraq, and whose fruits will only be judged in fairest fashion by history itself.

Therefore, I have exhausted all the immediate things that come to mind when thinking of the States. The summary of what I have described could be found in the adjectives: confident, crazy, weird, hurt and powerful. In short, these are the preconceived ideas fuelled mainly by my own television set.

2

Verbal Imprudence

On a beautifully calm October morning in 2003, I had taken my dog for a stroll in the local park to witness for the first time the dazzling richness of the red, brown, orange and yellow autumnal leaves that seemed, for some reason, to radiate with the most extraordinary *éclat*. As you will remember, the summer of that year had proved to be the hottest on record since temperatures had reached the 100 degrees Fahrenheit mark, thus causing the trees in autumn to put on the most fabulous display of multi-coloured leaves that rivalled in subtlety and variety the most diverse collection of delicate flowers. The morning really was a silent picture of arboreal contrast. Walking slowly among the trees, I bumped into a young neighbour of mine by the name of Amanda, who was also taking her dog for a stroll. We got chatting for a while and commented on the unusual serenity of the day.

'You know,' she said, 'This quietness makes me feel as though this is going to be the most boring day in a long time.'

'Why's that?' I asked.

'I don't know, maybe it's something in the air. It's just that, every now and again, you get really boring days when you can't find anything to do. That's why I took the dog for a walk, because I was so bored. I mean, what could possibly happen today?'

I immediately frowned on her last statement. 'You know,' I said, 'whenever anybody says anything like that, something usually follows.'

She looked perplexed. 'Sorry, I don't follow,'she said.

'It's just that the number of times I have heard someone say something like that, or take something for granted, the exact opposite of what they say nearly always seems to take place. It's a bit like a man who says, "I've been eating chocolate eclairs every day now for the past ten years, so I'll never get sick of them." Suddenly, he eats one the next day and becomes sick. Besides, I've got loads of stories like that, which lead one to choose one's words more carefully. For example, you said, "What could possibly happen today?" I mean, absolutely anything could happen, at any time, we just don't know. Anyway, I'm just telling you what I've observed, that's all.'

'Yes, but there's no way of explaining why the opposite happens, if what you say is true, is there? Unless, of course, you're the superstitious type.'

'As far as I know, I'm not superstitious. But there are people who believe in guardian angels and think that they listen to every word you say, and that whenever you take something for granted, they immediately knock you back in place. That is why the opposite of what you say happens, to teach you a lesson, I suppose, because otherwise you would become too arrogant. But anyway, that's for all people who believe in guardian angels.'

'Hmm. Well, I don't know about that, but anyway, you've got me interested enough to listen to your stories, if you don't mind telling them.'

'No probs.'

'After all, I have got time on my hands.'

'Okay.'

We began walking away from the trees onto a large grassy space.

'Right,' I said, 'I'm not going to recount every story, but I'll just give you two or three. The first one was in Italy twelve years ago. While still a student at university, I had gone travelling with a mate of mine around Europe. We had visited Holland, Germany, Czechoslovakia, as it was known then, Hungary, Austria, Slovenia and Italy. In the last country, we were nearing the end of our journey, since we were going to return to England after passing through France. In Venice, we were boarding the night train with the plan of crossing northern Italy from east to west in order to get to Nice in southern France.'

'And from there, you would both come back to England?'

'Yeah. Anyway, as we were waiting for the train to depart in Venice, James, my travelling companion, opened his mouth and said, "You know, Chris, this whole trip has worked out perfectly well, I mean, absolutely nothing went wrong, did it?" I naively agreed with him, not suspecting that his words may have been a bit imprudent at that stage. After all, we still had some distance to go. After his statement, we spoke a while longer and then settled down in our empty compartment to go to sleep. We woke up the next morning at Ventimiglia, the last Italian station before reaching the French border. Obviously, we all had to get our passports out, but the thing was I couldn't, because someone, in the middle of the night, had crept into our compartment and stolen my travelling bag containing my passport, money, credit cards and train tickets. At the station, I had to be interviewed by the police, who eventually allowed me to continue my journey to France after holding the train up for half an hour.'

'So how did you manage to get back without your documents and money?'

'Oh I had to go to Marseille to get a new passport, while borrowing money from a friend who lived nearby because James didn't have more than he needed for himself. But still, I could not help thinking of James' words the following morning when I woke up to find my travelling bag missing.'

Amanda seemed lost in analysis.

'The worst thing was,' I continued, 'that my friend's words seemed to backfire on me.'

'Yeah,' said my neighbour, 'it would appear that what your friend said was a little hasty in light of what occurred later, but still, I'm not saying anything, I'm just listening. So that was the first story, what's the second?'

'Right, the second story revolved around a speed-skater I saw on TV many years ago. He had been interviewed in front of the camera just prior to a major race. It needs to be said that he was a good speed-skater, having won loads of competitions before. In fact, I think he was the favourite.'

'But something happened, right?'

'Hold on. During the interview, he was asked how he felt. He answered by saying, "Well, you know, I've done this kind of thing so many times before and I've won so many times before that I'm pretty certain I'll end up on the podium one more time tonight."'

'That was a bit arrogant.'

'Exactly. Anyway, the race got under way. The speed-skater's usual tactic was to remain with the pack until the last lap and then suddenly break away, making a mad dash for the finishing line. As in all races, it's a very simple but effective tactic. So there he was, with the pack on the ice, getting ready for the final sprint when, totally out of the blue, he misjudged the tiny distance between him and a competitor in front and clipped the competitor's heel, which then sent him off balance and caused him to fly off in spectacular fashion at twenty-five miles an hour into the padded crash barrier surrounding the icerink. He was completely out of it and, again, I could not help but think of the words he uttered before the race.'

'So you're just saying that he shouldn't have taken the race for granted?'

'Precisely, because look what happened to him afterwards.'

'Well I'm sure he'll never say that again,'

'So now, do you see where I'm coming from?' I asked.

'Right, I tell you what,' said Amanda, 'give me your last story, then I'll tell you what I think, okay?'

'Okay. So then, the last story. This time, it was something that happened to me only two weeks ago on the bus. However, this time, it was not a question of what I said, but what I thought. Anyway, I was on the bus upstairs when suddenly I had the most imprudent thought. I was looking outside the window, observing the brilliant blue sky, and said to myself, "This year has been so good, what could possibly go wrong now?" Two seconds later, I got up off my seat to go downstairs and get off at the next stop.'

'And yet again, something happened, right?'

'Hold on. As I casually strolled down the aisle of the top deck, you have to remember that the bus, at that particular moment, was motionless since the driver was at some traffic lights waiting for them to go green.'

'Okay.'

'So I had to be careful because, at any moment, the bus was about to move forward once the lights had changed.'

'Yep.'

'The thing is, the thought I had made me become so complacent that I thought nothing of going down the steps. I put my foot on the second or third step when, at that precise moment, the lights changed. The driver put his foot down in such a way that the whole bus violently jerked forward with unusual force.'

'Oh my God, you had an accident?'

'Not quite, but I wasn't far from having one. As the bus jolted forward, my whole body was pulled backward and downward by the force of gravity. Obviously, you have heard it said, that for every action, there is an equal and opposite reaction. Had I not instinctively grabbed hold of the nearest railing with all of my strength, I am quite sure that I would have landed at the foot of the stairs in such a way that I would either have broken my neck or sustained serious injury.'

Amanda raised her eyebrows in shock.

'Yeah,' I continued, 'it was fortunate that it didn't happen but, I tell you, I almost kicked myself for having such a stupid thought.'

By this time, we had reached the most central part of the park, surrounded by the multi-coloured canopy of the trees in the distance. We stopped to have a look, while giving our dogs a brief moment off the lead.

'You know,' said Amanda, piercing the tranquillity, 'there might be one reason so far unmentioned that would explain all those stories you've just told.'

'Yeah, go on.'

'Well, it could just be that whenever someone says or thinks something imprudent, as you said you did on the bus, it simply affects your normal levels of judgement. For example, had you not thought, "What could possibly go wrong now?" maybe your levels of alertness would not have been altered. That's why you almost fell down the steps. I mean, the same could apply to the speed-skater, who became so complacent that it affected his normal performance. As for what happened to you in Italy, well, that could have just been that you left your travel bag in an unsecured place after hearing your friend's words. Otherwise, you would have been more careful. So I agree with you that what I said may have been a bit imprudent, but it's just up to me now to be careful for the rest of the day, otherwise you'd have me really worried.'

'Sorry, that was not my intention but, anyway, I've already given that idea some thought and the notion that things still remain in your control is almost definitely ruled out on hearing the story of the man abroad who was on the final leg of his journey. Suddenly, he said to his mates on the train, "Right, we can all relax now," only for the train to break down immediately afterwards. I mean, how could he have had an influence over the train's engines? But still, I see you're taking a more down to earth explanation of things, which is just as well. After all, I could be wrong. You never know, you might be right by saying that absolutely nothing will happen today.'

Just then, an enormous blistering sound came from the skies to the north of where we were standing. We both turned our heads then remained motionless, noticing that the dogs too had looked up to the sky. The eruption of sound seemed to be echoing in ever increasing volume as it was clear that the most electrifying experience was about to sweep us off our feet. Directly beyond the sparkling autumnal leaves of the oaks, sycamores, birches, pines and poplars, there appeared on the horizon a distinctive white form that I had only seen or heard about on TV. Its size grew rapidly bigger, while it emitted one of the loudest reverberating man-made sounds that must have easily reached the 120 decibel mark. It was Concorde. At this stage, there was no point trying to talk or shout, for there was no human voice able to override the noise produced by the Rolls-Royce engines. We could only stand and stare. As it happened, we were in exactly the perfect spot to witness Concorde stream above our heads at very low altitude. The dogs cowered on the grass, failing to find any refuge. The plane indifferently roared past in a display of combined might and elegance that would give any parents the most fantastic story to tell their children at bedtime. Overall, the experience was overwhelming. Little did I know that this was going to be the first and last time I would ever see Concorde in the air. Still, it pushed forward, apparently drawing the attention of all those onlookers within range of its sound. In the distance, people shielded their eyes from the brightness of the sky while trying to come to terms with the formidable sight above them. Soon, the sound dwindled as Concorde flew further south to then head eastwards towards the airport. All in all, the experience lasted about a minute and a half. I'm sure no-one will ever forget that day in the park.

'Oh my God!' shouted Amanda. 'I have got to go and tell Dad what I've just seen.'

She looked at me incredulously.

'Anyway, Chris, nice talking to you, but I've got to go. Bye.'

She grabbed her dog, put it on the lead, then marched off.

I was left asking myself why it was that Concorde had flown so low over the city of Birmingham. I later reached home to learn on the news that Concorde was being taken out of service and that, just before, it was flying around Britain with the aim of saying farewell to the country that had helped build it.

In the end, Amanda's prediction of the day in question was turned on its head to then give way to the most memorable experience in recent years. Her imprudent words had been proven wrong.

3

The Art of Sales

To discover the real craft of salesmanship, one needs only to look at the two following dialogues between a passer-by and a pair of competing fruit stall attendants.

'Hello, sir, how are you?'
'I'm fine, thanks.'
'Would you like to buy a fresh coconut?'
'Er, no thanks, I'm fine.'
'They're very juicy!'
'I'm sure they are, but I don't normally eat coconuts.'
'Well, they're good-sized ones, so you'll get good value for money.'
'No, as I said, I don't normally eat coconuts, so I think I'll pass on the offer, thanks.'
'Can I interest you in anything else?'
'Not really. Anyway, I've got to go, bye.'

'Now, sir, you look like the kind of person who hasn't tasted a juicy coconut in a very long time.'
'Well, actually, you might be right there.'
'Ah, the coconut. Big, tasty, ripe and excellent for adding a bit of the exotic to your daily diet. Doctors will tell you that there are many nutrients in only one single slice of coconut.'
'Yes, I suppose so.'
'So, if I were to make you a special deal on the price of these coconuts, so that for just £1.50 you can take three of them home with you for the kids, I'm sure you'd agree that it'd make a good alternative to the usual crisps and chocolate bars. After all, you know what kids are like with food nowadays.'
'Yes, I know what you mean. Okay, it sounds like a good idea, espe-

cially since, in the news, they're always going on about a healthy diet for kids. Right, I'll take them. How much did you say they were, £1.50 for three?'

'£1.50, sir, definitely the best deal you can get around here.'

'Very well, there you go.'

'Thank you, sir. You'll see, your kids will love 'em. All the best.'

It was during my time with a large commodities firm in London that I was taught the true principles behind selling an article to a customer on the phone, and I use the imaginary dialogues above to offer an insight into the do's and don't's of how best to approach the same person. I focus on a coconut because that was the precise object I was asked to sell in a group exercise designed to measure our compatibility in the field of sales on the very first day. Other people in the group were given a variety of objects, from a bottle of sun-tan lotion to a ball of elastic bands, with the same purpose in mind. Afterwards, our assessor would inform us individually on whether our performance was satisfactory enough to be admitted on to the full-time training course, and it was only there that I found out what qualities the assessor was looking for. These qualities can be spotted in the second dialogue.

If we start with the first, we immediately notice that the attendant fails to awaken the interest of the passer-by. He asks him rather direct questions that can only lead to a 'yes' or 'no' answer. On the training course, we were shown how such an approach would normally only yield a negative result. In fact, one could even term it a 'closed' approach where, as we see, the customer automatically refuses to be drawn in even though the vendor claims his fruit to be fresh and juicy. Somehow, the attendant's attempts to attract the customer simply do not work. On the other hand, the second stall attendant does not hesitate to build a rapport with the man. He invites him to appreciate the fruit's worth with a statement that can only lead to a positive answer. Compared with the first attendant, the second uses an 'open' approach to which the client cannot say 'no'. As a result, the vendor builds on this and homes in on the features, advantages and benefits of the coconuts he is selling. These three words are very important in understanding the talk of a salesman. If we are to take the second dialogue as a model for this technique, then we gather from the vendor's spiel that the feature of the coconut is its size, taste and condition. He also refers to its exotic nature, which then prompts him to comment on the fruit's nutritional element. Here, he is focusing on the advantage of eating a coconut, in that it offers dietary goodness. Still, the attendant does not stop there. He goes on to expand on the benefit of buying a coconut, since it will enable the customer's children to have a greater variety of food. Obviously, the client never told the attendant that he had children, but the latter raised the idea in such a way as to find out more about the person he was dealing with and, sure enough, the idea paid dividends, seeing that three coconuts were sold instead of one.

Therefore, it is evident that a lot of quick thinking and practice goes into making a good salesperson. Try it at home. Just grab the first thing that comes to hand and try and sell it to your family using the techniques shown. It is certainly an amusing exercise. However, it needs to be stated from the outset that some will find it comes naturally while others will not.

Thus, all is well when one sticks to the criteria of using the features, advantages and benefits of an object to sell it to a happy buyer. Yet, the moment one oversteps the boundary by using excessive manipulation to sell the product, one starts to wonder whether it really amounts to foul play. This was precisely the question I asked myself four days into the course, after coming under the impression that the business not only sought to exploit our talent, but also sought to exploit our own little minds. After three days of being bombarded with vast chunks of information regarding the history, products and statistics of the firm, we were introduced to a woman named Rachel whose task it was to engage us in the psychological side of things. She was tall, orange-looking (due to her fake tan) and spoke in such a way as to reveal her intimate knowledge in the field of sales. Despite her colour, she was the kind of person who you would buy from just to make her happy rather than doing so out of necessity. This was down to her excellent phone voice, which, she stressed, everyone in the field of sales should be at pains to master. She began by asking us to draw a picture of a pig.

'I know it seems strange at the moment,' she said, 'but it's just a way of getting to know each other a little better.'

We all complied. As we drew, a supervisor came over to check the kind of pig we were drawing. He looked over my shoulder and frowned in a somewhat perplexed manner. He immediately shot over to Rachel and whispered, 'That's really strange; that guy over there has drawn a full-frontal picture of a pig's face and body!'

Rachel remained quiet while coming over to see the image I had drawn.

'Right,' she said after a while, 'finish what you are doing and we will try to interpret the picture you have drawn. Ready? Okay. If you have drawn a pig facing the left of the page, that means that you are, arguably, a traditionalist. If, however, you have drawn a pig facing the right, that means that you're the kind of person who likes to experiment with modernism. Out of interest, how many of you have drawn the pig at the top of the page?'

Many in the group put their hands up.

'Okay, so that's good. That means that you are a positive person. For those of you who didn't, and drew your pig at the bottom of the page, that means that you tend to suffer from negativity and low self-esteem, so you're going to have to be careful, because here we all have to be positive. Still, there are ways of working on one's negativity and we will help you with that. Anyway, let's have a show of hands for those who drew a pig with a tail.'

Again, many of the group put their hands up.

'Right, that's interesting because it means that you enjoy a good sex life, although watch out for those who have drawn a pig's tail with a few curls in it; that means you're twisted. Otherwise, if you haven't drawn a pig's tail, that means you haven't got a sex life at all.'

Most of us laughed at these words but, in particular, a Jamaican girl next to me who noticed that my picture did not feature a tail.

Our orange-looking trainer then carried on reciting what each little feature on the picture meant, from the size of the head to the length of the pig's legs. Apparently, every little detail revealed an aspect of one's personality.

'What about mine?' I asked Rachel. 'Mine's neither at the top, nor at the bottom. It doesn't face right and it doesn't face left. What does that mean?'

'Hmmm.' came the reply.

Afterwards, we were all asked to put our name on the top of the page and hand it in, little aware that what we were, in fact, submitting was an invitation for our superiors to analyse our characters through this form popular psychology. Apparently, our drawings would make it all the more easy for the company to mould us in their image, if one pays attention to such an exercise. This idea was echoed in Rachel's following words.

'Now,' she continued, 'there is a reason for doing that. As I said beforehand, we'd like to get to know the kind of person you are. We are all different and we all have our strengths and weaknesses but, the thing is, you might not be aware of them, and that is precisely the objective of this training course; to find out what they are. Now, you could say that we're going to enter the psychological phase of things to make you the best salesperson possible, and I'm going to tell you a little story to tell you why psychology is important.'

'A few years ago, I was the kind of person who could have sold any-thing to anyone, whether they be little old grannies or hard-pushing businessmen. You name any object, and I could sell it. At the time, I was doing door to door sales and all went well until I set myself a par-ticular target. My favourite colour is the colour blue and, for some reason, while driving back home one night, I told myself that I would only knock on the front door of a house painted in blue. Don't ask me why, I just thought it. Now, from that time on, every time I saw a blue front door, I'd knock on it and try and sell my goods, no matter who answered. This carried on for a while but then I suddenly realised that what I was doing was illogical and that I had got myself into a rut. So I had to get out of it, and I could only do so with the help and support of my friends and colleagues. That's why it's impor-tant to remember that the same kind of illogical thinking could hap-pen to you. You could also get yourself into a rut, and that's why mon-itoring here is so essential. Now, everything you say and do here will be monitored by us for your own good. Somehow, you've got to recognise and take your good points and build on them, and we'll help you to do that, because you've got to remember that, in order to sell goods, you are going to have to change yourself. Whenever you talk to a customer on the phone, you are going to have to be a different person. But don't worry, because after the working day is over, you can go back to being yourself.'

These last words prompted me to think that being one person one moment and then being another at another moment was an excellent way of encouraging a personality disorder or, at least, an individual state of confusion. The group listened attentively to these sugar-coated statements.

'Anyway,' continued Rachel, 'we're now going to do another little exercise. Could you get up from your tables and form yourselves into a queue in the order of your dates of birth, disregarding the actual year you were born in?'

We all got up and assembled ourselves in the required fashion.

'Right,' she said, 'all those whose birthdays fall between January and March, assemble yourselves into one group at a table. Those from April to June into another. Those from July to September into another and those from October to December into another. We're going to mix you up a bit to see how you work in teams.'

I was about to settle into my group when she suddenly gave me and another man the choice of joining any team. The other automatically chose the one which contained a good-looking black girl, who he had tried to chat up all day despite already having a girlfriend. Now was the perfect time to chase his goal. I, on the other hand, simply chose the least boring group. Half an hour later, during the team exercise, Rachel went up to the budding Casanova to ask him openly why he had opted for that group.

'Well,' he grinned uncomfortably, 'I felt as though I knew this group already.'

He tried hard not to look at the black girl.

The lady in charge then came up to me and asked me the same question.

'Well, I had to pick some group.' I said, while concealing the real motive.

At this point, I suspected that these questions were a genuine attempt to uncover the motivational triggers behind our choice of group. This method of searching our inner-most thoughts led me to decide there and then to leave the course at the end of the day, for, indeed, if our strings were going to be pulled, no doubt we would have to do the same with our clients.

4

Being 'Right'

Very occasionally, a small wager is the best means of settling a dispute between two individuals who are both convinced they are right concerning a minor factual matter. As we all know, it is always nice to be right, and always humiliating to be wrong. Yet, there are some who can never be wrong, because to admit that they are so would damage their pride, and God forbid that such a thing should happen to them! Still, the following is a real-life example of how a person can fall into the trap of believing what they want to believe in order to have the last word of the day. It must be stressed that we are all guilty of such pettiness, and that it is a sure sign of maturity to be able to tolerate someone constantly in the habit of proving him or herself right, regardless of what the facts may indicate.

It was in the beer garden of a local pub that I entered into conversation with a young man by the name of Shane. We were among a group and our conversation focused chiefly on scientific issues. We spoke about human exploration and how man knew more about space than he did the sea or the centre of the Earth. Other members of the group listened while downing their beer.

'Yes,' said Shane, 'I saw a programme the other day on how difficult it would be for man to go to the centre of the Earth due to the present inefficiency of our technology, for while man knows a heck of a lot about the moon and outer space, he knows comparatively little about what lies beneath us. Quite simply, there is no machine or vessel capable of descending really deep into the Earth. In fact, there is no vessel capable of descending to the deepest part of the ocean, let alone the Earth itself, so that just about wraps that one up.'

Here, Shane was perfectly right about man not being able to penetrate deep into the Earth but somewhat mistaken about not being able to go to the deepest part of the ocean. I corrected him in what

I thought was a polite manner.

'What?' he said. 'You're telling me that a submarine has gone right down to the deepest part of the ocean?'

'I never said a submarine, I said a submersible.'

'And that it went all the way down?'

'Absolutely,'

'Well, I think you're mistaken.'

The group monitored our reactions closely.

'I assure you,' I said, 'that I am not mistaken, and that a submersible has most definitely reached the deepest part of the ocean in the Pacific a few decades ago.'

My conviction only served to increase Shane's disbelief.

'Well, I don't believe it,' he said, shaking his head authoritatively. 'Firstly, everyone would know about it and, secondly, no submersible could withstand the pressure so far below water. As for the point about it being done a few decades ago, I think you must be confusing things, because they wouldn't have had the technology then. So I think you are most definitely mistaken.'

For some reason, the group seemed to take his side of the argument. Had I not been 100 per cent sure of the claim I was making, I would have readily acknowledged Shane's perspective, not being a scientific man myself, but the point was that I had no doubts regarding the fact. On top of this, all eyes were on me as though forcing me to acknowledge defeat. There was only one solution.

'Right,' I said, 'well, it's at times like these that it's good to put your money where your mouth is. What would you say to a little bet?'

'You're on.' said Shane, unhesitatingly.

We agreed on a sum of money small enough to ignore if lost, but big enough to add weight to the dispute.

'You've lost.' said Shane.

'I don't think so,' I answered. 'I think you've lost.'

'Well, we shall see.'

'We shall indeed.'

'Yes.'

'Hmm.'

'Hmm!'

Rather than enter a negative game of verbal tit-for-tat, I asked him to meet me the next day in private so as to settle the matter away from the company of witnesses. After all, there is no worse thing than being proved wrong in public. Also, this was particularly relevant to Shane since I knew all along that he was mistaken. The reason for my own self-assurance was quite simple: at home, I had two separate sources of information relating to the adventures of Jaques Piccard and Don Walsh, who, in early 1960, had dived 11,033 metres down to the bottom of the 'Mariana Trench' in the Pacific. The name of their submersible was the *Trieste*, and it was built of hyper-strong steel to withstand the pressure of the water. They had descended to the deepest part of the world's deepest ocean.

The first source of information was in a geography book I read as a child and the second was in a more recent best-selling science-based book written by a very well-known author. The evidence was undeniably true. All I had to do was go home, get the books out and make photocopies of the relevant pages. Surely, this was proof enough that the deepest part of the ocean had been visited by men. Yet, for some individuals, what is presented to them black on white is not good enough to believe. It's almost as though some people have to witness things for themselves before accepting them as true. This was most certainly the case with Shane.

I saw him the next day and showed him the two sources of information. He read them thoroughly and then reluctantly gave me the sum of money agreed on. However, it was not to stop there. After a few weeks, in almost identical circumstances, we had both found ourselves talking about the same subject in the same beer garden with the same group. This time, Shane had acknowledged the claim that two divers had reached the bottom of the sea in a submersible, but not without expressing certain reservations. In fact, he had even admitted to being 'sceptical' about the whole issue. On hearing this, I immediately challenged him on what he thought was true.

'Shane,' I said, 'can I ask you a question? Do you or do you not believe that two men in 1960 went down to the furthest reach of the ocean?'

'Not really.' he replied.

'So, do you believe it was a hoax?'

'Yes.'

'Do you believe that men went to the moon?'

'Not really.'

'So, do you believe that was a hoax as well?'

'Yes.'

I stopped there and then, sensing there was nothing more I could do to convince him of anything I said. That was the end of the road between me and Shane.

To use the name 'a doubting Thomas' in this context is to ask oneself why certain people cannot accept what is presented to them black on white. Of course, we all have to be careful about what we read, for not everything written in print is true, but to deny an established fact its true status is to realise there are those who cannot suffer their views to be compromised on seeing the real picture. As a result, it is more convenient for them to see what they want to see, and to be 'right' about it, rather than acknowledge anything that does not fit in with their way of thinking. In sum, this would appear to be the pervading logic behind those, who, like Shane, always wish to have the last word.

5

Fear of the Unknown

There is no greater fear than the fear of the unknown. As it happened, I found this out while swimming off the southern coast of France in my early teens. During that period, it was customary for me and my family to go to a variety of beaches every weekend when temperatures soared in the summer, since, at that time, little thought was given to the dangers of sunbathing. Still, most people, when thinking of a beach, usually imagine a sandy one, gently caressed by the soft waves and accompanied by a refreshing sea breeze. Yet, when one considers a place by the sea on which to prop up a parasol and play with a frisbee in the sun, one realises that there are various kinds of beach.

In southern England, one can find pebbly beaches, with thousands upon thousands of smoothly surfaced, flat or round stones adorning the waterfront, while, elsewhere, one comes across a far more dangerous type of beach characterised by enormous chunks of flat and jagged rock holding its own against the smashing motion of the waves. It goes without saying that on these rocky beaches one has to be extremely careful where to penetrate the waters so as to avoid being tossed mercilessly between the crashing waters and the rock surface, and, for this reason, there are special entry points marked by short descending ladders bolted into the rock for maximum security. To dive from these areas is very risky, since the shallow waters are filled with sharp-edged stones and dotted with numerous sea urchins, whose tiny spikes would greatly hurt if landed on or trodden on. Therefore, it is wise for adults and children alike to wear specially made thick-soled plastic sandals in order to tread the seabed in safety while being pushed to and fro by the ever aggressive currents.

As can be imagined, this is a far cry from the relative comfort and leisure of a sandy beach, where little attention is given to getting off one's towel to cool down in the waters while frolicking with a beach ball. Indeed, small children on rocky beaches have to be constantly monitored by their parents, as accidents can all too easily occur, and it was on this particular type of beach in the Mediterranean that my family and I decided to spend one hot Saturday afternoon.

Settling down on a hard, flat surface, we laid out our towels, slapped on the suntan lotion and dozed off in the glaring sun. Around us, the beach was populated with other families either munching their picnics or gesticulating in conversation, while, occasionally, children would gather around rock pools to chase the small crabs scrambling about trying to find refuge in a cleft. I got up to join them but, after some time, went back to the family patch to whip out my plastic sandals and goggles. I was ready for the sea. I headed out to the waterfront, while paying close attention to the slippery moss covering the wet rocks. Here, good balance was of the essence. I reached the ladder and climbed down into the water. Savouring the cooler sea temperature, I waded through the shallow depths to then begin a good, healthy swim.

After ten to fifteen minutes, I prided myself on the fact that I had never swum out further than on that day. Nearby were a couple of serious swimmers, who ventured out towards the orange buoys. Looking at them, I wanted to do the same but thought I would take a peek under water beforehand to see what was there. After all, it was not every day that I dared swim out so far. I pulled up the goggles from around my neck onto my eyes, drew in a deep breath and went headfirst into the sea. At first, I could see nothing due to the stream of bubbles caused by my initial descent from the surface, but what became apparent to me once the bubbles had vanished made me shoot upwards in a desperate bid to get back to land. What I had seen within the space of five seconds was enough to scare the living daylights out of anyone not accustomed to the sea and I immediately promised myself never to swim out further than absolutely necessary.

The view that had filtered through to my eyes was both immensely beautiful and downright terrifying. Between me and the coast, and close to where I was, were tightly packed schools of small, roaming fish, whose various colours were lit up in fluorescent fashion by the sun's rays, alongside larger, more solitary predators no doubt waiting for the moment to pounce on their prey. The whole sea underneath was lit up in equal fashion by the sun, which produced a shade of blue similar to a clear sky shortly after dusk, and, behind the fish, one noticed the deep seabed, covered with every kind of sponge, coral or sea plant, growing silently amid the massive rocks, while bearing witness to the richness of life in the sea. The mixture of the blue colour of the water with the red, pink, gold, yellow and grey hues of the fish alongside the green, orange and cream shades of the seabed creatures created an impression that any artist would regard as sublime, and to capture the moment on canvas one would have to use the most diverse and subtlest oils while simultaneously expressing the tranquillity of the blue depths. Arguably, it was one of the most fabulous displays of 'artistry' I have ever seen.

However, what I saw with dreaded fear was not the picture of life just touched on, but what lay directly beneath me. As mentioned, one could see the rocky seabed leading out into the waters away from the coast, but it has to be clarified that this gently sloping seabed was, in fact, an enormous rocky shelf that, at some point, had to come to an abrupt end. I had dived at precisely the right place to witness what lay at the end, and I never want to see it again. What I saw made me understand why some people are afraid of the sea, and what I saw was this: at the end of the rocky shelf came a perfectly vertical cliff face that plunged precipitously downward into the far reaches of the Mediterranean. This may not sound like much, but at that moment in time, it seemed to plummet downward in stark defiance to any land dweller who set eyes on it, and that land dweller was me. As the cliff face descended, I grew acutely alarmed at the ever darker waters shrouding it in mystery and menace. In short, I had been confronted with the unknown, and I did not like it. I was suspended above the abyss in perfect fear of what lay below and the desire to rejoin the land could not have been any greater.

On reaching the surface that particular day, I swam back as quickly as I could, climbing out at the shallow waters. I returned to my family, where I was given a Camembert sandwich. I ate while evoking the thought that if ever I was given the choice between going down to the bottom of the sea, or going into outer space, I would most surely choose the latter, such was the fear inspired by the unknown depths off that rocky beach.

6

Animals and Us

While on safari in southern Africa, I had come across the peculiar sight of a rhinoceros contemplating the thought of ramming our vehicle. Being in an open-top safari van with a group of English lads, we had stopped a while to observe a herd of white rhinoceroses in close proximity, who seemed rather indifferent to our presence. Yet, there was one who seemed quite alarmed at being watched. He left the herd to observe us closely, about thirty metres away. The rest of us went quiet, with some members taking pictures of the animal in front of them. The rhinoceros then lowered its head, while keeping the van securely in its sight. Its stance resembled that of a rugby player eyeing up the posts before taking a conversion. It took two steps forward and then scraped the ground with its front left foot, while snorting loudly and viciously. His head began bobbing up and down as though counting down the seconds before drastic action was taken.

'Shit. It's gonna charge.' said one group member, peering through his binoculars.

'Nobody move!' directed our African guide at the wheel.

I myself was setting up a contingency plan in my mind to decide whether I would stay in the vehicle or jump off in the case of a full rhinocerotic assault. A slight breeze blew through the blades of tall savannah grass around us. Otherwise, the scene was a perfectly still one. The creature's head then remained motionless. For a few long seconds it seemed lost in thought, debating whether ramming the vehicle was a worthwhile enterprise. Suddenly, its stance became more relaxed and, after a few seconds more, it headed back towards the herd. The danger was over, but it was interesting to have a glimpse of an animal appearing to ask itself, 'Shall I, or shan't I?'

It was after recounting this story to a colleague of mine at the local

31

pub that we began exchanging views on whether animals are indeed capable of reasoning like us or, at least, whether they are able to do so on a smaller scale. I took the view that they did not, while my colleague, Jim, argued the contrary.

'My dear friend,' he started, 'animals must have reason. Firstly, your story of the rhinoceros in Africa would suggest that he was thinking of something; what, we do not know, but he was thinking of something. And, secondly, I could tell you the story of something that happened down under that proves that animals are capable of reasoning.'

'Okay, I'm all ears.' I said.

'Not too long ago, in the newspaper, I read the story of a family who went swimming in the sea somewhere off the coast of Australia. All went well for a while and they were enjoying their time in the water. Suddenly, to make things even better, they were surrounded by several dolphins. They all frolicked around for a while but then the family grew alarmed that the dolphins would not allow them out of their circle. Every time a family member tried to get out, a dolphin would immediately push them back in. This went on for an hour or so. Suddenly, for some reason, the dolphins allowed them to swim back to the beach. It was only afterwards that the dolphins' behaviour was explained. Apparently, in those same waters was a great white shark. The dolphins, aware of this fact, were protecting the family. That, my dear friend, proves that animals have reason in that the dolphins had to work together to save the family. There's no way you can deny that.'

I remained quiet for a moment, taking in the story before answering. Jim's eyes glimmered with the conviction that he had proven his case. Finally, I gave my response.

'Okay, I admit it's a very beautiful story, but couldn't it be argued that the dolphins were acting out of a protective instinct rather than out of reason?'

'Protective instinct?' said Jim. 'No, I don't think so. I think it's safe to conclude that they acted out of reason because they must have all communicated the same idea among themselves. So, if they have a language, they must have some reason.'

At this point, both our voices were becoming slightly raised.

'Hold an a sec, hold on a sec,' I repeated. 'Who said anything about animals having an actual language?'

'Oh, c'mon, everybody knows that. I mean, you must have heard the language of dolphins on TV. Everybody has!'

'Yes, but is it a language that revolves around words?'

At this, it was Jim's turn to be silent.

'I mean,' I continued, 'I see what you mean, in that animals have their own form of communication in much the same way that a dog barks or a horse neighs, but I think we know that their "language" cannot be compared with ours in any way as far as words are concerned.'

'But that's because we haven't discovered their language yet.'

'Believe me, if man can unravel the mystery of the Rosetta Stone, written in Greek and in Egyptian hieroglyphics and dating back over 2,000 years, then man is most certainly capable of deciphering the language of the animals, if there were such a thing. Unless, of course, you are saying that their language is so much more complex and advanced than ours that they, in some way, might be considered higher than us?'

'No, I'm not saying that, but what I am saying is that an animal is capable of some reason, and that it has a language of sorts.'

'Hmmm.'

Rather than continue our conversation on the animals, we decided to call it a day agreeing that it was very difficult to reach a compromise between us. Still, I do believe that our discussion created a footing on which to base the difference between human and animals and which can be discussed here in further detail.

It may or may have not escaped your notice that my conversation with Jim contained two key words that may go a long way to distinguishing ourselves from beasts. Those two words are instinct and reason. Humans, as well as animals, have instincts, the most beautiful and powerful of which is the maternal one, as most people have experienced that indefinable bond that draws a mother to her children. Therefore, following one's instincts in this sense can be very good. Yet, on another level, we humans also have the capacity to ignore them, or not to follow them at all, which may be less evident in other creatures. For example, a person who is on a serious diet will choose not to eat his or her favourite muffin on the table despite having the urge to do so. An animal, on the other hand, will not be able to help itself, if it has the chance. On being hungry, it will almost certainly tuck in to fulfil its instinct, since there is nothing in its mind to stop it. This behavioural comparison would suggest that a human can exert reason over instinct, thus controlling it and channelling it in the appropriate way. That is why the question of language is so important, in that it reveals the articulation of reason rather than basic instinct, while making us conclude that the communication of animals revolves around instinct rather than reason. Still, this is not to say that the animals are far more impoverished than us in terms of their capacity to live, for after all, their instinct may be far more developed than ours, but an instinct will always remain an instinct and nothing more as far as the beasts are concerned.

Just to add a little weight to this whole theme, I quote the words of René Descartes, the seventeenth-century French philosopher widely regarded as being the father of modern philosophy. As you may already know, he was the one responsible for the expression, 'I think, therefore I am',[*] and it is from the same work, *Le Discours de la Méthode* (1637), that the passage is taken:

> Now... one can also recognise the difference that exists between men and animals. For it is quite noticeable that there are no men, so slow or retarded, or even bereft of all sound judgement for that matter, who are not capable of assembling together several words, or expressing speech that enables them to make known their thoughts. However, there is no other animal, so perfect, and so perfectly endowed, that can do the same. This is not a question of lacking the necessary organs because we know that magpies and parrots can also articulate words like us, but at the same time, they cannot do so in the sense of demonstrating any thought-related utterance.

---

[*] Here, might it not be argued that 'I am, therefore I think' is a more appropriate statement, considering how a human can only reason several years after being born? However, that is taking us in another direction altogether.

Conversely, those men, who, having been born deaf and dumb, and who in some way, may be equally or more deprived than the animals in terms of the organs used for speech, are in the habit of inventing for themselves signs through which they can communicate to companions who have the leisure of learning their language. Therefore, not only does this show that animals have less reason than men, but that they do not have any whatsoever, for one knows that very little reason is needed to be able to talk. Further, upon examining the inequality spread among animals of the same species (as also occurs among men), with some being easier to tame than others, it is not conceivable that the most perfect parrot or monkey of its kind rivals in this regard the most stupid child, or at least, the most mentally affected one...

Here, Descartes is making a very clear distinction between animals and us, in that the most wonderfully formed creature cannot in any way be compared to the least-gifted individual regarding reason or language. While taking this point onboard, it is interesting to observe how a person, on constantly repeating the words or views of others, might be termed a 'parrot', thus reflecting the idea that the person cannot think for him or herself. It is needless to say that this expression is derogatory, but it clearly shows that one is expected to demonstrate a certain level of individual thought that no animal can possibly emulate.

So far, we have dealt with the most striking differences between beasts and men in terms of language, reason and instinct. Yet, there are two more questions that have remained untouched. The first is whether the former are able to conceal their instincts or feelings in the way that a human can. It is often heard that man is a 'complex animal', but it is not often explained why. I personally believe that the answer to this statement lies in the fact that a human can easily hide all those interior emotions that play a vital role in everyday existence. An animal, it may be argued, cannot, for we know that a dog, on being happy, does not give itself the choice of not wagging its tail. If it is happy, its tail will wag. If the dog is not happy, its tail will sink towards the ground. Hence, a human, in theory, should be far more difficult than a dog to read, if that person decides to keep to himself all those thoughts, emotions and feelings rather than divulge them to the exterior. One can even say that a man or woman can speak aloud without letting on their true intentions, whether this be a matter of convenience, deception or avoidance. Therefore, it is certainly with good reason that we are known as complex animals, notwithstanding how a cheetah in the wilds will crouch behind grass or bushes to pounce on its prey, thus, making us aware that they too are capable of a certain kind of deception. Still, at the same time, we know that it can only do so through instinct.

And last but not least is the one important question concerning the complete lack of artistic ability in animals, since it is wholly apparent that none whatsoever have ever sought to reproduce their surroundings on canvas or in any other way. Why is this so? It may have something to do with a greatly inferior sense of consciousness, for if one looks at the cave paintings of Lascaux in southern France, one realises the degree to which, at some point, man must have become so aware of himself and the environment in which he lived that he took up drawing on walls as an outer expression of that inner awareness. After this, one simply remains baffled at how the transition from ape to man could have ever taken place without an exterior force of some kind instilling a sense of beauty and art in the latter, and, not surprisingly, that is where one begins to enter the sphere of religious belief.

Ironically, I end with the only serious account ever written about a rational and talking animal found in the Book of Numbers in the Bible. Although written very factually, it demonstrates to all those who believe in the Bible that God is even capable of making a donkey speak like a human. However, that, and all the rest, I will leave for you to evaluate.

7

Noise Pollution

Over a decade ago, while still in my late teens, I had the opportunity of saving my next-door neighbour's life, which, I hoped, would prove sufficient reason for him to turn down his music late at night. The only times I had ever spoken to him before were often after midnight, on the steps to his front door, telling him in plain and polite English that his Irish folk music was too loud. Half the time he was drunk and argued violently that his music was not too loud and that he had a right to do whatever he pleased. He would then slam the door in my face, to then shout obscenities through the wall before switching his TV on to the same volume until three o'clock, when he went to bed. Indeed, these are the inconveniences of living in terraced housing. The point was that he could not comprehend the stress that constant loud music or television can cause to those who like a little peace and quiet. That is why, on coming back from shopping one Saturday afternoon and on perceiving that his house was full of smoke, I took it upon myself to see whether a charitable action was enough to make him finally listen to my plea.

Outside his front door were two young nephews of his who seemed perturbed that their uncle did not answer the doorbell. They looked through the letterbox to notice something strange going on inside.

'Excuse me,' said one of them, 'I think my uncle's house is on fire.'

'Are you sure he's in?' I asked.

'He's supposed to be. That's why we came.'

I came round and peered through the letterbox to see thick grey smoke pervading through the neighbour's front living-room.

There was no time to lose. Action had to be taken.

'Right, wait here.' I said.

I immediately went round into an alleyway running behind the house, climbed over the back fence and ran to the kitchen door leading out to the garden. I turned the handle, but it was shut from the inside. At this point, there was only one thing I could do, which, with hindsight, gave me untold delight after years of suffering noise pollution and sleep deprivation from my neighbour. That was to smash his door in. This was a perfect chance to vent all that closed-up anger caused by someone too insensitive to take others into account, while, at the same time, doing him a favour. The feeling was brilliant. Still driven by the urgency of the situation, I began kicking in a large wooden panel near the base of the door with the idea that I could climb in afterwards. The sound of my shoes repeatedly beating the door reverberated through the whole house, as it took about thirty seconds to finally knock the panel out of place. I crawled in. Having got this far, it came to me to prepare myself for any eventuality, since I had never before had to deal with a domestic fire. Yet, as soon as I lifted myself off the kitchen floor, a distinct smell told me that the direct cause of the smoke was not a fire but, rather, some overcooked kippers. Coughing and spluttering through the dense fumes, I found exactly what I suspected on the gas cooker; a couple of charcoal-coloured fish in the middle of a large frying pan. I took them off the fire to be suddenly accosted by the occupant.

'What's going on?' he asked, somewhat dazed.

I explained. He shook me by the hands, opened the window and told me that he had fallen asleep on his sofa for an hour while forgetting about the kippers. The sound of my kicking the door in had woken him up.

'Don't worry about the door,' he said, trying to catch his breath, 'I'll take care of it.'

I immediately interpreted this last statement as a tacit acknowledgement that, in future, he would be more careful regarding the volume of his home entertainment, which was confirmed by an unprecedented period of tranquillity at night for the next two weeks. During that time, I had allowed myself to believe that the same man had at last managed to exercise control over the loud noise he so desperately liked to hear.

Therefore, going to bed one late evening, I put my head on the pillow and began tucking myself in for a good night's sleep. Suddenly, out of the blue, came the slightly muffled but unmistakable sound of a battle scene being watched on television by the man next door. The music of the film worked in perfect conjunction with the booming of canons and the screaming of soldiers. In the dark, I opened my eyes fully aware that the period of tranquillity was over.

In France, there is a saying that has a perfect relevance to the topic of noise pollution, and which is encapsulated in the following words: 'The freedom of one ends with the freedom of another.' This simply implies that as soon as one person decides to indulge him or herself in whatever they please, very often the well-being of another is automatically compromised. This, in turn, denotes the propensity of many to put their own pleasure before the rest, which then reveals to us the very core of their self-centred philosophy. To people such as the annoying Irishman (and quite a few neighbours after him) the concept of self-restraint is a very unfamiliar and vague one. It is almost as distant and alien to them as Outer Mongolia. They do not understand that sometimes the best way to nurture diplomatic relations in society is to practice harmless self-abnegation: and just as distant and alien to them is the language or concept of compromise. How their little minds readily scurry away from such an idea. Time and time again, like a recurring theme, it is as if the same idea were perpetually entering through the narrow orifice of one of their ears only to navigate aimlessly about the empty parts of the brain to then be quickly blown out at the other side lest it dare drop anchor. As with a mathematical constant, the neighbour next door will under no circumstance change and in this case, offer safe port to that thought which says: 'When you live with others, you have to think of others.' Instead, the man or woman in question hardens him or herself into an unalterable state of egocentricity, while becoming in the process a puerile, noise-polluting pest. Moreover, and whilst forever yielding to the temptation of fixing the volume control to mind-bendingly annoying levels, he or she must think: 'Suffer ye, my weary and protestant listeners, as it is now time for me to revel in what you dread the most day in and day out, for it matters not to me whether you must endure tiredness at work on my account, or even whether you lose your job as a result, because, as far as I am concerned, the music I play at ungodly hours is all about me, me, me, and moi, moi, moi, so there!' Therefore, any immediate sense of compromise is discarded from the outset. For example, is it that excruciatingly painful to turn down one's volume to more modest levels or find a pair of powerful earphones instead of forcing neighbours to potter about the house all day with spongy earplugs stuffed half-way up their auditory canals? Apparently so. The fact is that most of us love music, but when next door neighbour's deep bass resembles the accompanying drum beat to siege works trying to ram the inner framework of one's mind, one instinctively feels like severing all previous friendly communications. The result is a perpetual atmosphere of contempt between the parties concerned, which is why the Irishman could not help but shout things like 'Bastard!' across the wall after I had repeatedly asked him to be more quiet, while another young Asian neighbour took the liberty of tipping trash in my front garden and fully relieving his bladder on the front door to my house soon after I asked him to turn down his reggae rhythms. These are merely people who cannot fathom the elegance and practicality of self-denial, choosing instead to sow misery in the lives of others. Indeed, how far apart are the philosophies of Epicureanism and self-restraint on this strange planet of ours.

Add to that the element of power. Take the recently arrived black African family living on the other side of the house and the unemployed English youth now residing in the former home of the Irishman. Both are very ordinary people in the strictest sense of the word. Yet, place a megawatt hi-fi in front of them, and their eyes will glimmer at the prospect of switching the 'ON' button, for they subconsciously realise that this apparatus will fling them into a position of power over neighbours when they turn the volume upward, while escaping the monotony of ordinary life on regarding loud sounds as a vehicle to their own self-aggrandisement. Consequently, I, the neighbour in question, am obliged to live my life on their terms as I am often woken up in the morning by the vivacious beat of Latin-American music, played on my right by the Africans, to then spend the whole day suspecting that, in the evening on my left, the English youth donning a baseball cap will pump up the volume with his rampant techno. Seemingly, you can't win, because if power is the ability to impose on others what they wouldn't otherwise endure voluntarily, then those noisy neighbours have certainly got the upper hand. In short, they are tyrants in their own pathetic little 'right'.

Yet, to take things just one step further, one notices how this exercise in power fast reaches excessive proportions as victimised neighbours are often forced to become refugees in their own home. 'I know,' says one family member, trying to placate the others by finding a practical solution to the ongoing problem, 'let's go to the front living-room, it might be quieter there.' Immediately said, everybody gets off the sofa to embark on a mini procession from the second living quarters to the first in the hope of finding peace. Once there, all realise within no time that the pounding music emanting from the difficult person's hi-fi next door penetrates just as deeply as in the second living-room. 'Okay,' says another, 'well, let's all go to the kitchen.' Again, once there, the same thing happens only for the procession to lead everyone upstairs. On the landing the family gathers with each member rapidly turning into a desperate scout on a mission to find an area free from the ever intrusive noise. They all go into the bedrooms but come back shaking their heads. There is no escape. Now, having come to terms with the futile quest, there remains one more option which should have been the first to be considered rather than the last, and that is to go on a nice litle excursion to the nearest bobby house to lodge yet another complaint. The family listen one last time to the ludicrously loud rhythms played next door to see whether the neighbour has in any way attempted to down the volume. He or she hasn't. 'Right, out we go.' says one, with a distinct tone of suppressed anger reflected in the voice. The door is slammed behind them for the noisy neighbour to inwardly delight at what has been accomplished. And all that at the neighbour's touch of a button.

But what about the sound diffused by television? In many ways, it can be equally, if not more, testing than that churned out by the loudspeakers of stereos, and especially so after midnight. To begin with, there is the constant stopping and starting of loud, bleary conversation, with the exact phonetic definition of words partly cut out by the exasperatingly thin walls. Instead of making out the words, one notes with remarkable distinction the tones of the televised characters rising and falling in the style very particular to English. Here, one recognises whether the scene is romantic, dramatic or other and, for a long, drawn out period of time, one is destined to suffer largely unintelligible and fuzzy conversation. Suddenly, there is a moment of reprieve in the form of silence. These silences are like tiny drops of gushing fountain water sprayed in the air during an oppressively hot summer's day. As a result, you want more, but at the back of the mind, you know you'll have to content yourself with very little. In vain, one urges the silence to perpetuate itself, hoping that the neighbour has at last thought better than to watch TV and has gone to bed. Yet, as always, the moment of silence is broken by either adverts, music or a fast-paced action sequence, thus reminding you of your neighbour's unwavering indifference. And this is where one has no other choice but to go knocking on his or her door. Needless to say, this is also the point where hostilities may easily commence.

All that goes to demonstrate how, today, we live in a world of noise, from people cranking up the volume of their car stereos to others elsewhere who cannot do without upsetting their neighbours day after day with the unremitting sound of blaring music systems. Hence, if we are to take the expression 'An Englishman's home is his castle', then we are made well aware that his castle is, at present, being besieged by an unprecedented flood of noise, which, in the view of many, should be tackled by better-defined limits on the noise produced by a neighbour. In the same way that there are stringent speed restrictions on cars, I am sure that many 'victims' of noise pollution would also welcome a more direct approach with loud music, but who, for the time being, simply dream of living next door to a little old granny who does nothing more than silently spend her time performing the gentle and peaceful art of embroidery.

8

Theological Brain Cells

Sometimes, it is important to stimulate the old theological brain cells. Everyone of us, at some point or other, must ask ourselves why we are here. I know I do. As someone once told me, 'Very often, people who cross deserts, lands and countries, and things like that, ask themselves the reason to everything.' If I were to fall into a certain category of person, I would probably fit into that one.

As it happened, while going to Bosnia by coach, I came across an inadvertent argument for the existence of God in a book called *A Short History of Nearly Everything* by Bill Bryson. It's an interesting book, dealing with a whole range of subjects from the Big Bang to particle physics, in a way that is very clear and accessible. It is probably the most interesting book on such matters since even I was fascinated by what he said on chemistry, a subject that I usually have no interest in. Therefore, the work certainly has some merit. However, at the beginning of a chapter entitled 'The Rise of Life', Bryson explains how seemingly impossible it was for life to begin in the first place:

> In 1953 Stanley Miller, a graduate student at the University of Chicago, took two flasks – one containing a little water to represent a primeval ocean, the other holding a mixture of methane, ammonia and hydrogen sulphide gases to represent the Earth's early atmosphere – connected them with rubber tubes and introduced some electrical sparks as a stand-in for lightning. After a few days, the water in the flasks had turned green and yellow in a hearty broth of amino acids, fatty acids, sugars and other organic compounds. 'If God didn't do it this way,' observed Miller's delighted supervisor, the Nobel laureate Harold Urey, 'He missed a good bet.'

Press reports of the time made it sound as if about all that was needed now was for somebody to give the flasks a good shake and life would crawl out. As time has shown, it wasn't nearly so simple. Despite half a century of further study, we are no nearer to synthesising life today than we were in 1953 – and much further away from thinking we can. Scientists are now pretty certain that the early atmosphere was nothing like as primed for development as Miller and Urey's gaseous stew, but rather was a much less reactive blend of nitrogen and carbon dioxide. Repeating Miller's experiments with these more challenging inputs has so far produced only one fairly primitive amino acid. At all events, creating amino acids is not really the problem. The problem is proteins.

Proteins are what you get when you string amino acids together, and we need a lot of them. No-one really knows, but there may be as many as a million types of protein in the human body, and each one is a little miracle. By all the laws of probability proteins shouldn't exist. To make a protein you need to assemble amino acids (which I am obliged by long tradition to refer to here as 'the building blocks of life') in a particular order, in much the same way that you assemble letters in a particular order to spell a word. The problem is that words in the amino-acid alphabet are often exceedingly long. To spell 'collagen', the name of a common type of protein, you need to arrange eight letters in the right order. To *make* collagen, you need to arrange 1,055 amino acids in precisely the right sequence. But – and here's an obvious but crucial point – you *don't* make it. It makes itself, spontaneously, without direction, and this is where the unlikelihoods come in.

The chances of a 1,055-sequence molecule like collagen spontaneously self-assembling are, frankly, nil, It just isn't going to happen. To grasp what a long shot its existence is, visualise a standard Las Vegas slot machine but broadened greatly – to about 27 metres, to be precise – to accommodate 1,055 spinning wheels instead of the usual three or four, and with twenty symbols on each wheel (one for each common amino acid). How long would you have to pull the handle before all 1,055 symbols came up in the right order? Effectively, for ever. Even if you reduced the number of spinning wheels to 200, which is actually a more typical number of amino acids for a protein, the odds against all 200 coming up in a prescribed sequence are 1 in 10^{260} (that is a 1 followed by 260 zeros). That in itself is a larger number than all the atoms in the universe.

Proteins, in short, are complex entities. Haemoglobin is only 146 amino acids long, a runt by protein standards, yet even it offers 10^{190} possible amino-acid combinations, which is why it took the Cambridge University chemist Max Perutz twenty-three years – a career, more or less – to unravel it. For random events to produce even a single protein would seem like a stunning improbability – like a whirlwind spinning through a junkyard and leaving behind a fully assembled jumbo jet, in the colourful simile of the astronomer Fred Hoyle.

Yet we are talking about several hundred thousand types of protein, perhaps a million, each unique and each, as far as we know, vital to the maintenance of a sound and happy you. And it goes on from there. To be of use, a protein must not only assemble amino acids in the right sequence, it must then engage in a kind of chemical origami and fold itself into a very specific shape. Even having achieved this structural complexity, a protein is no good to you if it can't reproduce itself, and proteins can't. For this you need DNA. DNA is a whiz at replicating – it can make a copy of itself in seconds – but can do virtually nothing else. So we have a paradoxical situation. Proteins can't exist without DNA and DNA has no purpose without proteins. Are we to assume, then, that they arose simultaneously with the purpose of supporting each other? If so: wow.

And there is still more. DNA, proteins and the other components of life couldn't prosper without some sort of membrane to contain them. No atom or molecule has ever achieved life independently. Pluck any atom from your body and it is no more alive than is a grain of sand. It is only when they come together within the nurturing refuge of a cell that these diverse materials can take part in the amazing dance that we call life. Without the cell, they are nothing more than interesting chemicals. But without the chemicals, the cell has no purpose. As Davies puts it, 'If everything needs everything else, how did the community of molecules ever arise in the first place?' It is rather as if all the ingredients in your kitchen somehow got together and baked themselves into a cake – but a cake that could moreover divide when necessary to produce more cakes. It is little wonder that we call it the miracle of life. It is also little wonder that we have barely begun to understand it.

By referring to amino acids as 'the building blocks of life', we stumble across the building blocks for a creationist argument that life could have come from none other than a divine entity. What other than the finger of God could have put together millions upon millions of rightly ordered proteins to build a fully functioning you or me? The answer is simple; nothing else could have. It is mathematically impossible. As alluded to in the above extract, things just do not have the habit of assembling themselves, ever. The idea of a cake's ingredients coming together to somehow bake themselves is one of many examples that could be used to put forward the creationist point of view. Among other things, one could mention the idea of a helicopter or a car miraculously piecing all its components together to suddenly come alive with vibrant energy. All it would need is for someone to fly it or drive it. As any person of intelligence will know, this simply will not be. Instead, every component will have to be methodically placed, one by one, over a period of time, until the article is finished. This applies to everything, from a pair of basketball boots to a pair of sunglasses. For anything to work properly, *everything* has to be pieced together. This is where the idea of a Creator comes into play. In the same way that a person weaves a carpet or manufactures a teddy bear, God must have assembled all of His Creation. In this light, one might even call Him the 'Great

Assembler', putting everything in just the right place and giving it life. In a sense, there is nothing to understand except that life is a miracle and that a miracle is, by definition, inexplicable.

'It seems strange that in this day and age, people still believe in God,' a young man in England once said to me, 'especially since evolution explains everything.'

'Does it?' I asked.

'Well, yes,' he answered, quite vehemently.

'So how do you explain the formation of the eye, then?'

'What do you mean?'

'Well, don't you think it's a little bit strange that the eyes should suddenly form themselves?'

'Yes, but we're talking about their formation over a period of millions of years.'

'Even so, it doesn't explain how eyes can gradually form themselves.'

'Yes it does.'

'No it doesn't.'

'Well, you are wrong!' he snapped. 'Evolution explains everything.'

'Except the eye,'* I finished.

What we were, in fact, touching on was a nineteenth-century theological notion that plan precedes purpose. In other words, that everything that is ever made has to follow a blueprint before the time of its existence. This applies to humans as well as to cars, aeroplanes or trains. Before building a house, for example, a plan has to be devised in order to envisage where every brick will go. Needless to say, building something without a blueprint to precede it will inevitably lead to a dilemma, especially if we are talking about something complex. We are no different, and the formation of the eye suggests that only a superior intelligence could have given shape to it. Remember that the eyes have many different components to them, from the lens, to the retina, to the photo cells at the back. Not

---

* Even Darwin, the great man himself, could not account for the formation of the eye.

only that, but we are talking about two eyes, each one working together in conjunction with the brain to form the image we see. In a fashion, we are a complex set of machinery, artistically engineered to go about our daily business. The only question that remains to us is to ask who made us.

'Oh man, I believe, I believe that at midnight on the eve of the year 2000, aliens are going to descend on the site of the Pyramids. They're gonna come back to the place they left centuries ago, 'cos, let me tell you, they're the only things that could've made us.'

This was voiced to me eight years ago by an American tourist in Greece after I had told him that I planned to go to Egypt.

'Really?' asked an Australian girl who was listening to the conversation.

'Absolutely,' he replied. 'Have you ever heard about DNA? It's totally awesome. I mean, it's so complex that only extra-terrestrials could have programmed it. Yep, you better believe it, aliens are definitely gonna land at the Pyramids!'

As far as we know, this has not happened.

I, personally, do not believe in aliens. This may come as a shock to many, who, like the American and the Australian above, are readily given over to such an idea. Regardless of the statistical probability that intelligent life may exist elsewhere, there arises a theological problem that needs to be addressed. Would that intelligent alien civilisation be contaminated with Original Sin? If not, wouldn't we be doing them a disservice by wanting to get into contact with them? Original Sin obviously goes back to the creationist belief that God made the universe. As we know, God expelled Adam and Eve from the Garden of Eden for having disobeyed His command not to touch the Tree of the Knowledge of Good and Evil. Whether you believe in this or not, the story would certainly explain the existence of evil that we find all around us. For this reason, then, it would be very important to realise that by contacting supposed aliens, we would be exposing them to the disease of Original Sin. It would be reminiscent of the Indians contracting smallpox from the white settlers after the discovery of the Americas. Besides that, believing in aliens does not account for how the universe was made in the first place, for one could also ask how they themselves came into existence. I think that people who like to believe in a more advanced extra-terrestrial civilisation tend to be people who have an ardent (but misplaced) desire to search for what is greater than them. After all, we are beings with a limited capacity. Isn't it normal to search for what is beyond us? That is why religion is logical in that it grants us permission to express ourselves to that great fundamental mystery: God Himself.

Another point I consider worthy of mention is that not only is our universe and world structured and orderly but it is also artistically composed. Go anywhere in the wilderness and you will notice that it is beautiful, from the dazzling whiteness of Antarctica, to the golden sand dunes of the Sahara, to the great grassy plains of North America. Surely, we would not want it any different. Look up into the night sky and you will see a whole array of glittering stars clustered into varying constellations. No-one can tell me that that isn't beautiful. One could even say that a human artist does not create anything; he simply copies what is already there. For example, a landscape painting is merely a representation of what the artist saw. So how did everything become so randomly beautiful? It is my conclusion that it didn't – it was made that way. Indeed, seeing for-eign lands and countries does make you question everything.

So, in this way, were my theological brain cells triggered into motion by the long extract in Bill Bryson's *A Short History of Nearly Everything*. Apart from that, the book is brilliant for boosting one's general knowledge. Did you know, for example, that an atom is only one ten-millionth of a millimetre long, or that Yellowstone National Park in America is a giant caldera volcano that could explode at any minute? Nor did I until I read the book. Still, I close with the memory of an Indian carpet seller in Italy who voiced to me in three simple words what he thought on the topic of belief: that 'God is fact.'

9

Language Learning

It was during my first trip to Spain at the age of twenty that I realised how horribly inefficient I was at understanding Spanish, despite having learned it for the previous three years. Speaking it was not a problem, for I had assimilated all the necessary grammar, vocabulary and expressions, but taking aboard other people's spoken words proved a task so difficult that, in the end, I would often pretend to understand what they said rather than run the risk of upsetting them through my blatant lack of comprehension. This would happen all too frequently. A perfect example was in Madrid, where I was hoping to contact a Spanish friend by the name of Paco, who lived in Badajoz. Unfortunately, I had lost his phone number while still retaining his home address. It was my intention, for the purpose of knowing where to go next, to ring up an enquiry line to see if I could obtain Paco's number. After all, I was not interested in waiting the extra week it would take to write to him and receive a reply. The only way I could contact him was by phone. I entered a phone booth and dialled the enquiry number. The operator answered and I explained to her what I was looking for. She immediately churned out a fast, long-winded statement full of rolling Rs and sibilant Ss. I didn't understand a word. I asked her to repeat herself. She did so in exactly the same style. My mind went blank: I simply could not formulate her words in my head. I asked her to repeat herself again more slowly. The operator exploded on the other end of the line.

'What on earth is wrong with you? I've already told you twice! What is this, some kind of joke?'

That bit, I managed to understand.

'I'm sorry,' I said, 'it's just that I'm English and I don't understand very well.'

'English? With an accent like yours? Rubbish. I am sick and tired

51

of these prank calls. In future, don't waste our time!'

She hung up.

Somehow, one is better able to understand a foreign language when things get personal. Still, I walked out of the phone booth asking myself why it was that I could not string together the most basic dialogue spoken by other Spanish people around me. The answer was simple: this is what happens when you only learn a language with a book.

It is entirely true that speaking a language is one thing, while understanding it is another. From my own personal experience, it would appear that some have a far greater aptitude for the former rather than the latter, and vice-versa. For example, if I were to give myself marks out of ten for my ability to speak compared to my ability to comprehend, the marks would be eight and two accordingly, which is hardly more advantageous than someone who was marked five and five. Therefore, one has to grasp how learning foreign words from a page has a completely different effect from learning words directly from the mouth of a native speaker. As a result, we come across two methods of language learning that lead us to ask which is most relevant for the serious student of modern foreign languages. I will start with the written form.

For some, like myself, to see a word on a page invites an instant memorisation of the same word via the image-producing part of the brain. Thus, the word is lodged and stored in the cerebral areas dealing with sight, memory and linguistic knowledge. That is why when you see the same word written elsewhere, you will immediately understand its meaning, because you have recognised it visually. In this way, many words can be learned quickly for those who are visually minded. Yet, while assimilating rapidly, there is one major drawback that confronts the individual when applying that linguistic knowledge to the audio part of the brain. Sometimes, the connection is too faint and this is precisely why I had great difficulty in understanding many Spanish people. Obviously, this was not something I could explain to the operator on the phone. In short, learning Spanish from a book did wonders for increasing my knowledge of the language, but practically nothing to tune in to its phonetic qualities, despite being able to imitate it verbally. Like on a radio, I simply could not find the right frequency for verbal comprehension and it is here that we grasp the importance of learning a language principally by ear. It must be stated that adopting this method is far slower than learning words on a page, but in the long run, your ability to tune in to the frequency and communicate with foreigners will be greatly enhanced since the method used is based primarily on the way a baby is taught to speak.

If one thinks about it, a new-born child does nothing but absorb information from every new colour to every new sound. His or her brain is like a tiny sponge soaking up all the new data received from the surroundings. Then, very slowly and mysteriously, the brain starts making sense of what the child sees, hears, touches, tastes and smells. The same applies with language. Little by little, after hearing the same series of words over and over again, the baby will subconsciously associate an object with a word to then be able to string short sentences together by the age of two or three. It is as if the child's mind is on autopilot. With this, every parent or guardian witnesses the natural linguistic capability most children have. What's more, they will understand clearly most of the things you tell them to do or not to do. Normally, it is only after this stage that they begin to read and write, but by then, their brain will be fully processing all the audio material that penetrates their ears and it is this that cannot be duplicated by learning foreign words on a page, no matter how gifted you are at languages.

Hence, the pure listening method is by far the most advantageous and efficient way to progress linguistically, which is why there is no replacement for one to one tuition with a 'native' or repeatedly hearing a foreign language on tape, despite the deep feeling of boredom and monotony the latter may produce. Altogether, and from my experience, the written should complement the audio and not vice versa, since otherwise it is a bit like speaking into a phone without hearing the person at the other end. However, it is enough to know that most language courses today use a combination of both written and audio skills to ensure maximum progress for the student.

10

Spookiness

On going down to the local newsagent's several years ago to buy myself a packet of ten Berkeley Menthol cigarettes, I got chatting to the shopkeeper, who was a good person to know when it came to finding out all the latest gossip in our area. Thus, many a time would our conversation touch on whose house was occupied by drug addicts or prostitutes to ensure that I avoided them on my way back. However, on this occasion, we touched on the topic of the various films we had seen at the cinema.

'Well,' I started, 'I've seen *Spiderman II* and *I, Robot*. Not bad films altogether.'

'Yeah, me too,' he replied. '*The Day after Tomorrow* isn't a bad one either. It's good when you haven't actually got a baddy in the film. I mean, when the weather hits you, there's nothing you can do, is there?'

'Nah, I suppose not. Apart from those two or three films, I haven't seen much else, apart from *The Passion of The Christ*.'

'Oh. *The Passion of The Christ*,' he said, somewhat morosely.

'Have you seen it?' I asked.

'Yeah, yeah, I saw it, but I didn't think much of it. I mean, I had heard so much about it that one day, I just went. I didn't like the spooky parts, but I suppose the rest of it was okay. It's just a shame they put the spooky parts in.'

'What spooky parts?' I ventured to ask.

'You know, that evil-looking man with the black hood.'

'Oh, the devil, you mean?'

'Yeah, that's right. I didn't like those parts. To be quite frank with you, I don't know why Mel Gibson bothered putting that in there.'

'Yeah, but can't you see; he's trying to put onto the screen the constant battle between Good and Evil, which is not an easy thing to do. The only thing he can do is put in a pale-faced man with a black hood to represent the interior struggle that goes on in all of us. I mean, you and me, for example. What Mel Gibson is trying to portray are interior realities that are relevant to everyone.'

'Well, whatever. I didn't like the spooky parts.'

I left the shop shortly afterwards seeing the conversation had disturbed the shopkeeper.

In a certain sense, Mel Gibson's *The Passion of The Christ* is one of the most realistic films ever made. Far from seeking only exterior realities, it also explores what goes on in the most hidden recesses of every individual. Jesus Christ, apart from being presented to us as the Son of God, was not excluded from the drama that takes place on a day to day basis in the hearts of men. To exclude his inner struggle with the devil would be to portray him as a two-dimensional character. No. *The Passion of The Christ,* in all its cinematographic gore and vivid detail, invites us to reflect a while on the temptation Christ endured for us right up to the moment of his death. It would have been easier for him to say, 'No, I don't want to go through that', yet, for our sakes and the good of man, he accepted the chalice of suffering allowed to befall him by his Father. In this sense, therefore, does Mel Gibson's film accurately bring home the inner torment that would otherwise be hard to express.

Apart from that, one also realises that *The Passion of The Christ* touches on levels of extraordinariness. Firstly, there is Jesus, whose identity was not an ordinary one; he claimed to actually be the Messiah. Secondly, there are the Pharisees, whose wickedness towards him surpassed any 'normal' level of malevolence. Thirdly, there is the staggering indecision of Pontius Pilate, who eventually gave way to the request of the Pharisees to have Jesus executed. Finally, there is the extraordinary physical suffering of the man whose messianic identity was the reason used by his people to condemn him. Thus, the miscarriage of justice was extreme, to say the least, or even demonic. That is why it was necessary to include the character of the devil, in order to fully grasp the truth behind Christ's torment. One only has to look at the beaten, bloodied and battered figure of Christ to capture this. However, if there was one thing even more extraordinary than all these details, it was the Resurrection itself.

On a more emotional level, and on having watched Mel Gibson's rendition several times at the cinema, one noticed a number of spectators either weeping silently, laughing loudly or walking out in sheer disgust. True, the tearing of flesh and the sadism of the Roman soldiers is not for the faint-hearted. Still, there was one character whose presence brought forward a compassionate and loving heart, without which the madness of Calvary would have been unbearable to watch. That loving heart was found in the person of Mary, the mother of Jesus. Amid the insults, spittle and the jeers heaped upon her son, she saw for herself the diabolical influence of the man in the black hood. She was tuned in to the atrocity of her son's death. Here, one has to be acquainted with the Catholic interpretation of the Scriptures in order to directly understand Mary's role as regards the salvation of men. Otherwise, in *The Passion of The Christ*, she offered the only thing she could give at the time: motherly warmth. In this light, then, can Mel Gibson's film be considered an extraordinary cinematographic venture, and it was this aspect that the shopkeeper I spoke to failed to recognise.

11

Presumption

While a student at university, I had gone down to the basement of a hall of residence to wash and dry my clothes. Already there were two more students doing the same thing. I duly put my clothes in the washing machine, subsequently taking them out to dry on the washing line. To pass the time, we all conversed on our own subjects of study. Suddenly, out of the blue, one of them, named Jerry, pointed out a certain aspect of my jeans on the washing line.

'You see that, there?' he asked.

'Yes,' I said.

'That's a crease.'

I remained motionless for a brief period stunned by Jerry's statement. Did he really believe that I had never seen or heard of such a thing? He spoke in such a way that indicated his seriousness on the matter.

'A crease?' I asked in bewilderment.

'Yes, a crease. You see that line running away from the seam? That's a crease. Look, you've got another one there, you see?'

His friend said nothing, but seemed aware of the surreal nature of the situation. After all, here was a younger student than I getting it into his head that I had never come across the word 'crease'. I decided to play along with Jerry's pedagogy to see just how far he took my ignorance.

'Oh, I see!' I exclaimed. 'That's a crease, then?'

'Yeah,' replied Jerry, 'you see, whenever there's a fold in the material, it causes the material to bend and crease. That's why you have to use an iron, to iron out the creases.'

'Oh, an iron? Yeah, I think I've heard of that thing before. Isn't that a kind of handle attached to a flat metal base that one has to heat before pushing over clothes?'

'Yeah, that's right, although you have to be careful with an iron, otherwise you might burn yourself.'

At this point, I dropped the play acting, realising there was something seriously wrong with this person's perception of me. What was he going to tell me next, my own name?

'Jerry,' I said, 'I'm sure that you're a very nice person, and that you've got a lot of things to teach others, but out of everything you've just told me, I have learned absolutely nothing. All the best.'

I then walked away, noticing the friend shake his head dissaprovingly at Jerry.

To understand such an extraordinary case of human misinterpretation, one would have to delve into Jerry's thought processes to work out why he treated me like an ignoramus. One concludes that, somewhere along the line, he presumed that I did not know what the word 'crease' was. Still, he did not stop there. He then proceeded to act on that presumption, making me feel as though I was born yesterday. Therefore, his perception of me acted in direct accordance with his presumption. Then again, one has to ask oneself where the presumption stemmed from. In Jerry's case, did it come from the idea that he made a snap judgement about my outward appearance or character? Probably. However, this way of thinking reveals a certain logic that fails to take into consideration all the facts before acting acting on them. If this is true, one could term this logic or way of thinking as being rather two-dimensional. Unfortunately, we have all been in situations where our actions or words have been misinterpreted as a result of another's presumption and I think it is safe to say that it occurs on a daily basis more or less everywhere. Conversely, one is often forced into making a snap judgement about someone else, which may sometimes be amusing, but which may sometimes lead to more serious consequences. The following is another true-life scenario between myself and a friend in London that, on the surface, may not propose much, but which, if one digs deeper, will reveal quite clearly the kind of false logic alluded to.

Sharing a house with others on the outskirts of the capital, I had been offered the chance of applying for a new job by my friend,

Sharon, who also lived with us. She had brought over a party of work colleagues and told me in front of everyone that there was a position going at her imports and exports office. She beamed victoriously on admitting that her office was looking for someone who spoke French and Spanish.

'You speak those languages, don't you?' she asked me, with a grin.

'Yes.'

'Well, now is the perfect time to apply.'

She noticed my evident lack of enthusiasm.

'I do take it you want the job,' she said rather loudly, pushing the point home.

The group awaited my answer in silence.

'Not really,' I replied, shaking my head.

Sharon's jaw fell to the ground. She must have spent all day telling her mates that I would most definitely take the job. They, in turn, cast their eyes up into the air, not knowing where to look.

'Oh, he's only joking,' said Sharon, desperately trying to save the situation. 'Anyway, let's go into the garden, it's a nice day today.'

I remained indoors, avoiding any more difficulties with Sharon.

A few days later, she waited for the appropriate moment to pounce on the theme of my refusal.

'You know,' she snapped, 'you really embarrassed me the other day in front of my friends. Don't you ever do that again!'

From that time on, our rapport dwindled.

On analysis, one can work out the logic Sharon followed which proved the basis for her presumption that I would say 'yes'. Her thought pattern must have been: he will take the job that requires French and Spanish. Why will he take the job that requires French and Spanish? Because he himself speaks French and Spanish. Although there is a certain level of reasoning here, it does not take into account the fact that I already had a job, and that I was happy in it. It also failed to recognise that I would not normally envisage a job in imports and exports since it does not appeal personally to me. These were the reasons why I said 'no', but Sharon had not committed herself to searching out the truth. She simply took her presumption as fact and acted on it, which led her to feeling embarrassed.

After all this, one may still ask oneself why I deem it necessary to try and penetrate the thoughts of others. Let me just say that, after being a victim of so many people's presumptions on so many occasions, I have been forced to ask myself whether the fault lies with me or with them. Hopefully, this chapter on presumption will offer an insight on those people's thoughts and explain why I once had the displeasure of having French translated to me in public by a person who knew perfectly well that my first language was French, while being told on another occasion who Marco Polo was even though everybody knows he was a thirteenth-fourteenth-century Venetian traveller who went to China and, finally, being on the receiving end of a suggestion that the music I play on the piano is none other than the music I heard from inside my mother's womb, even though my mother is quite adamant she has never heard my compositions before. For, if such a thing were true, the chances are that I would be playing TV jingles from the early 1970s. These and many, many more reflections have been made about me, and no doubt, many more are to come. Still, it just goes to show how far from the truth people can go, while demonstrating how many individuals there are who think in that way.

12

Earthquake

It was on the night of 23rd September 2002, at precisely 12.54 a.m., that I actually felt the earth move beneath me. All those who recall that date will remember it was the night Birmingham was shaken by a mild earthquake, whose epicentre was in Dudley and which measured 4.9 on the Richter scale. I distinctly remember the episode and, for the sake of adding a little body to this chapter, it might be of interest to recount in small detail the event of the night in question.

Watching TV in the living-room at the aforementioned time, I suddenly realised that the coffee table in front of me began rattling steadily. The noise of the cups on top resembled the chinking of glass and cutlery on a ferry ship during docking manoeuvres. Here, it must be clarified that every passing fraction of a second became thick with critical apprehension. The thoughts I had came and went within an instant and it was as though the tremors had pushed with one fabulous stroke the spinning top of one's imagination to revolve incessantly on its axis. Around it went, generating an acutely alert stream of consciousness as one battled to remain the master of one's anguish, for one's mind, when not accustomed to unknown phenomena, immediately seeks reassurance by trying to grasp the truth behind the disturbance. Meanwhile, it frightened me to notice that not only was the coffee table shaking; it was the whole house. My mind whirled into action in an attempt to settle my fears. 'Is it the neighbours?' I asked myself, for very often, those next door would turn their hi-fi music quite loud. 'No, it can't be them because there's no music.' I reasoned. Then it came to me to think of an articulated lorry passing by in the street outside. However, there was no Doppler effect. The house continued rumbling in silence. Curiously, I remembered a highly bizarre bird call echoing through the trees an hour earlier, while taking the dog for a stroll. I had never heard that sound before and, indeed, its eerie cry resembled some strange sound effect created on the set of a horror movie. 'Does that have anything to do with it?' I wondered.'* Then I thought of the community outside. The community. That word very rarely sprang to mind, but there I was, considering belting it off the sofa to go and search out the company of the usually indifferent neighbours. Somehow, in times of catastrophe, the strength of numbers does much to soothe one's nerves. Yet, for some reason, I was not too sure whether to scarper outside or ride out the crisis by myself. I stood up in a general state of panic. Then came the most incredible experience I have ever had: beneath my living-room floor, I could feel the slow motion of enormous chunks of rock shifting in heavily grinding fashion. I knew it was deep below my feet. My fears were slightly alleviated when I finally found the answer: it was an earthquake. I waited for another ten to twelve seconds with my heart pumping wildly; then, suddenly, the vibrations stopped. That was an experience I will never forget.

This is all to say that the worst part of one's house rattling during a tremor is the utter sense of insecurity it inspires. Normally, in otherwise peaceful moments, one regards one's home as a place of refuge, a place of tranquillity where nothing should touch you. There you are, in front of the gas fire, warm, comfortable, at ease and at leisure. You go to the kitchen and make yourself a cup of boiling tea. You sip it and relax on the sofa to watch TV. The cares of the world are everywhere except in your living-room, and that's just the way you like it. Perhaps more alluring is the thought of going to bed one winter night to the sound of heavy raindrops outside. There you are, under a thick, cosy duvet, seeking the most comfortable position to set your body off to sleep, while listening to the rain pelting down on the window panes. Secretly, you are saying to the rain, 'I know you are there, outside, but I am here, inside, in the security of my own little home, and there is nothing you can do about it.' How that feeling of inviolability is swept away during an earthquake! Mother

* Could this bird call have been indicative of the restiveness of animals before an earthquake? I do not know because the dog never batted an eyelid during the whole evening. Still, it is interesting to note faraway reports of fish jumping out the coastal waters of Japan just prior to a major terrestrial disturbance in that country.

Nature, as though rudely awakened from her pleasant slumber, seems to recall those small words to riposte with a fraction of the might at her disposal. She answers by saying, 'Yes, I know what you thought, but remember, I am far more powerful than you know and, due to me, what you have today can easily be taken away tomorrow.' At this, a person cringes at his or her own insignificance as the house dwelled in is assailed from beneath. All one can do is fear and respect this power that no man can ever hope to tame.

Back in the living-room, I slipped on my shoes and raced outside to confirm with anyone who cared to listen what I had suspected. As I looked around, bedroom lights were flicked on and front doors opened for a small stream of neighbours to come trickling out into the early hours. Those who remained indoors had either slept through the earthquake or chose to keep to themselves. The youngest of children clutched their mothers' dressing gowns, while questions were asked and conversations started with all of us temporarily brushing aside our differences to welcome the individual concerns of the other. My Iraqi neighbours also came out but stood unperturbed in front of their bay windows. One lit a cigarette and I approached him to ask the burning question on everybody's lips.

'Did you feel it?'

'Of course, my friend,' he answered.

Another Iraqi mentioned something to him in Arabic and stared at me.

'My friend says you look afraid.'

'Of course I'm afraid, everybody is.'

'There is nothing to be afraid of, my friend. Where we come from, there are always earthquakes. You get used to them.'

'Yes,' I said, 'but in England, we don't normally get earthquakes.'

Behind me came a neighbour from a few doors up. He was tall, thin and in his pyjamas. I had never spoken to him before but I could see he was shaken.

'My God! Did you feel that?'

'I think we all did.' I said, half-jokingly.

'What was it?'

'An earthquake.' I replied.

'An earthquake? Thank God for that; I was watching this really spooky film on BBC2, when suddenly the whole house began shaking. It felt like the devil himself was trying to rip through the floorboards!'

'No, don't worry, it was an earthquake.'

'Thank God for that!'

At this, he turned on his heels and headed straight back inside. I have never spoken to him since.

The rest of us stayed chatting in the street for another half an hour, with people darting in and out of the front door to grab their coats. Then began the time for all to retire. Little by little, front doors closed and lights went out only for the latter to be switched on again two minutes later.

Other people had various interpretations as to what had occurred on that night. Some thought it was an atomic bomb, some thought it was a plane crash, while others had come to the conclusion that it was a huge mineshaft caving in from beneath. All this was made apparent on the news the next day during which a newsreader seemed rather surprised at the fact that anything at all could happen in Dudley, Birmingham.

Still, immediately after the earthquake, and from a purely sociological perspective, it was remarkable to witness the complete absence of indifference from neighbours who were ordinarily in the habit of ignoring you (and who had done so over the previous ten years). During that period in the street, no-one felt like a stranger and it was as though all barriers had come down. Instead, everyone was eager to communicate, listen and entertain in the best way he or she could, and, to a certain degree, it gave a positive slant to a very rare spectacle. Like the curtains on a Punch and Judy show, they were quickly drawn open to reveal the personalities behind the silent veil. Finally, after years and years of living in the neighbourhood, one got a glimpse of the real characters hiding behind the usual face of nonchalance. In effect, the earthquake had pushed all of us out of our shells. Yet, almost as soon as the curtains were drawn open, they were closed again, and, the next day, all went back to ignoring one another. At the end of the social gathering in the street, one felt like saying,

'See you at the next major disturbance.'

The same thing happened several days after the 7/7 bombings in London when an engine part under the bonnet of an old car mysteriously blew up on the side of the road. Again, this time on hearing a massive 'bang', neighbours trickled out (in greater numbers than before) to see what the problem was, which was natural. Fire engines came and police cars pulled up to ascertain whether there was anything untoward. There wasn't, but at the same time, one noticed the social barriers coming down between everyone. However, as soon as the commotion was over, all returned to ignoring you and to going their separate ways. Human nature is a funny thing, and we are all prone to behave in the same manner, but one can understand why people look to strangers when hit by a potential catastrophe: to find shelter and security in the company of others.

Meanwhile, the chief aim of these descriptions is to underline how it is entirely one thing to hear or read about disasters taking place in foreign countries, but quite another to actually live through them. One often sees reports about a tornado ripping through parts of Oklahoma or a hurricane blasting its way across the Carribean, but the moment the report finishes, so too does most people's interest. This is because we cannot fully personalise the facts. If, on the other hand, you or a relative were somehow caught up in these disasters, only then would you begin to relate to the event. It is logical. That is why anyone reading this chapter who did not experience the earthquake of September 2002, or any other earthquake for that matter, might not be able to relate to the above account. I know I never gave earthquakes a second thought before being shaken by one. If you think I am over-emphasising the issue, just remember that if ever you saw the ground open up in front of you during an earthquake, your chances of having a heart attack would rise significantly, such is the fear it would produce.

Therefore, using this as a basis for understanding the forces of nature, one can only stagger in disbelief at the powers unleashed on the Boxing Day earthquake of 2004, which resulted in huge tidal waves sweeping across the Indian Ocean and ended with the deaths of over 250,000 people. To even attempt to describe the individual and collective fear it provoked is beyond the capacity of most. I am not going to try it. Needless to say, there are many stories of death and survival which will have traumatised many, and it is only from this perspective that I can write about it.

Yet, if there was one thing to have shone through amid this seismic tragedy, it was the generosity of the world, whether financial or humanitarian, during the aftermath of the disaster. Despite the fact that most of us did not live the experience or suffer the torment of being engulfed by gigantic waves, we could relate on a human level to all those brothers, sisters, wives, husbands, fathers, mothers, sons and daughters who lost their lives on Boxing Day. Somehow, it touched us. And we gave. For, in the end, we realised that humanity is just one big family. We have our differences, certainly, but if there was one thing I personally found out during the weeks following the Boxing Day earthquake, it was that the world has a heart.

13

Human Choice

Working upstairs in a certain nursing home one morning, I did not
venture to ask a girl why she had mysteriously vanished from work
over the previous seven days. I used to live next door to her and simply presumed that she had been sick. The rest of the staff also wondered what she had been up to. Suddenly, however, while washing a
resident in the shower, she invited me to probe the reason behind
her absence.

'God, I feel like crap this morning. I should have taken another
week off work,' she said, shaking her head.

'Why, are you ill or something?' I asked.

'I've just had an abortion, haven't I? The doctor told me to take
at least another week off work, but I need the money. God, I feel like
crap!'

I said nothing but continued washing the patient. Before me, the
girl in question had told someone else and, before long, everybody
knew why she had taken a week off. Later, I went downstairs to the
kitchen to make some teas for the residents. There, was a happy mid-
dle-aged cook who seemed all the jollier that morning. We spoke
briefly on what we had heard and, after frowning, she used the
occasion to whip out a small image she was carrying in her white
overalls. She handed it to me in silence. It was an ultrasound picture
of her unborn grandson.

'My daughter's going to call him Luke.' she said. 'The image was
only taken the other day.'

I looked at the picture, drawing in my mind the significance of the
two contrasting stories upstairs and downstairs.

'No wonder you look so happy.' I said to the cook, handing her
back the image.

She said nothing, but smiled blissfully at her future role of
grandmother.

Afterwards, it was my custom to go for a lengthy cigarette break in the smokers' room, where I was joined by another care worker by the name of Shameel, who was pretty, petite and liked to engage in friendly, philosophical discussions, depending on her mood. She was Asian and was the kind of person to listen and assimilate rather than speak openly about her opinions, which made her someone who understood more than she let on. All this despite her evident lack of background education. For example, she did not know who Shakespeare was until I told her. Indeed, how curious it was to find someone who, on the whole, possessed more understanding than knowledge as opposed to the more common disposition of possessing more knowledge than understanding. Still, we sat down and began talking about the morning's events. I could tell she was in the mood for a deep discussion.

'You know,' I said, 'this morning was the very epitome of human choice.'

'What do you mean?' asked Shameel, with keen interest.

'Well, on the one hand, you've got the girl upstairs who decided to abort her baby and, on the other, you've got the cook's daughter who's waiting for the birth of her son. One person chooses death, the other chooses life. That, for me, is human choice in a nutshell.'

Shameel chose to remain silent for a while as I puffed away on my cigarette.

'I mean,' I continued, 'if you think about it, you spend your whole life making decisions whether you like it or not, from what you have for breakfast in the morning to the colour of your brand new car to who you marry. It's a bit like an ant climbing a tree.'

'Would you care to explain what you mean?' asked Shameel, politely.

'Well, if you can imagine an ant at the foot of an enormous tree, then you realise that once it starts climbing it's going to come across many diverging branches. Every time it comes across a new branch, it has to decide which way it wants to go. Does it carry on upwards, or does it choose to follow another branch in another direction?'

'Hmm, I see what you mean.'

'And you have to realise that the decision will keep on

coming again and again and again, until the ant goes as far as it can. And then, if the ant does decide to branch off, it'll have to go through the same process time and time again with regard to the smaller branches. All it is doing is deciding which route to follow.'

'But what happens when it gets to the top of the tree or at the end of a branch or twig?'

'Well, I wouldn't take it too literally, I'm just trying to explain how human choice works, that's all. I mean, we're not ants and we're not climbing trees. I'm just using an allegory.'

'What's an allegory?'

I explained.

'Anyway, coming back to what I was saying, sooner or later, the main trunk of the tree will split up and diverge in two completely different directions and it is up to all of us, whether rich or poor, black or white, man or woman, to decide which way we are going to go. You can either go one way or another; there's no in-between. In short, you have to decide whether you are going to lead a good life or a bad life. That is what the parting of the trunk signifies. It's the biggest decision anybody can ever make, because both will have serious consequences.'

'How do you know all this?'

'I spend much of the time thinking about things. In fact, you could even call it a hobby of mine.'

'Would you say that your travels have helped you form your opinions?'

'I suppose so, why do you ask?'

'Oh, I don't know. I just wonder, that's all. I mean, what did you actually discover on your travels?'

'I can sum it up in one phrase: the existence of evil. Nothing more, nothing less, which is why I'm saying that we each have to choose between good and evil. In short, that's what every human life is geared up to, because animals certainly can't make that decision.'

'But I thought you said ants have to choose which way they want to go?'

'I was using an allegory, Shameel, an allegory, you know, that word you didn't have in your vocabulary.'

'Oh yeah, I'm sorry.'

'But anyway, if you think about it, everything we're talking about goes back to the Garden of Eden.'

'Adam and Eve, you mean?'

'Yeah. What I'm saying is that, before the couple chose to touch the tree of the knowledge of good and evil, they had absolutely no awareness of what it was like to succumb to the bad. They lived in perfect freedom. The thing is, the devil seduced them to eat of the forbidden fruit, which then opened their eyes to the knowledge of evil. As a result, they became slaves to their own knowledge. Hence, their perfect freedom was compromised because there is no freedom outside God.'

Shameel's eyes narrowed with concentration. I continued.

'Which then begs the question: what is knowledge without truth? Because you can be a victim of knowledge, but not of the truth.'

Shameel looked at me blankly.

'Sorry, I'm trying to understand,' she said, shaking her head.

'I know you are. Don't worry, it's a rhetorical question.'

'What's that?'

I explained.

'Anyway, coming back to what I was saying, knowledge of good and evil is a bit like smoking, although on a more significant scale.'

'Smoking?'

'Because once you know what it is like to smoke it is very hard to give up the habit. Why? Because you have *knowledge* of what it is like to smoke. That's why, if you don't smoke, don't start. It also applies to other things.'

'Have you ever tried to stop smoking?'

'Yes, but, as I said, it's hard, because you are constantly being tugged in two directions. On the one hand, you want to stop smoking, on the other, you want to carry on smoking, and the same goes with the knowledge of good and evil; on the one hand, you want to do good, but on the other, there is always the temptation to deviate from the good. The only difference is that, once you stop smoking, the urge to light up disappears after a few weeks, whereas with temptation, it is always there to lead you astray and it sometimes

72

takes a real effort to resist temptation. Basically, you've got to choose whether you resist temptation or not, because life is just a battle with yourself. I mean, we're all made up of good and bad, or black and white, or whatever you want to call it but, the thing is, in the long run you have to decide which will take the dominant role in your life, because, by giving in to the good, your saying "no" to the bad, and by giving in to the bad, you are saying "no" to the good. There's no two ways about it, whatever people may say. Thus, the story of the ant who has to choose which way it wants to go.'

'But what if the ant doesn't want to choose?'

'It has to choose; it has no choice about not choosing.'

'What?'

'I mean, it's a bit like people who say that they didn't choose to be born. They're right, they didn't choose to be born; they simply were born, but what they don't understand is that it's not a question of choosing to exist, but choosing how to exist, because, in order for God to ask you whether or not you wanted to exist, he would have to make you beforehand. It's logical. But the thing is, once he's made you, he chooses to maintain your existence whether you like it or not. Therefore, you can only choose how to exist after you're born.'

'And what happens to the person who constantly chooses to have a bad life?'

'It's quite simple really, if a person persistently chooses to lead a bad or immoral life without ever turning back to the good, because we can always choose to become good if we want to, that person will go to the fiery furnace down below.'

'My God, you don't honesty believe that, do you?'

'I most certainly do because in the end you know whether what you are doing is right or wrong. I mean, it all depends on the exact degree of awareness you have concerning right or wrong, because sometimes, our minds can be clouded with uncertainty regarding certain things. But if you know full well that you are doing evil to others, or in any other capacity, and if you persist in those actions without ever turning back from your ways, you will go where I mentioned, which is why I say one person chooses life and one person chooses death. In short, the person who chooses the good chooses life and the person who chooses the bad chooses death. That is the very epitome of human choice.'

'Hmm...' said Shameel, stroking her chin.

'I mean,' I said, 'I'm not talking about fairy tales or Santa Claus or things like that, I'm talking about reality. Take, for example, the woman the other day who told me in a hotel bar, in front of others, that I should get off my "big fat arse" and see the world and do something with my life. Well, I've already got off my "big fat arse" and seen the world. I mean, I've been to about twenty or so countries but, in the end, you just have a choice to make; you either become a sheep or a goat. There's no in-between.'

'What did you tell the woman?'

'Well, on telling everyone that she was going to Ireland for three months, I told her that once she got there she should keep heading westwards, no matter what she found. Then I left.'

Shameel laughed but then asked me about heaven.

'No-one knows what heaven's like,' I answered, 'which is interesting because many have a good idea of what below's like, but no idea about heaven. The thing is, you can't describe heaven because it's a bit like trying to describe to a blind man who has never seen colours what the different colours of the rainbow are; he simply won't have a clue as to what those colours look like. It's impossible. So, basically, you just have to give God the benefit of the doubt and believe that heaven is a great place, for lack of better words.'

'You're certainly comfortable up there in your thoughts, aren't you?' replied Shameel.

'Well, we've all got to decide what life's about at one stage or another. The question is: who has the right interpretation?'

'Can I ask you a question?'

'Shoot.'

'How can you be so sure that evil exists?'

'Can I in turn ask you another question? Do you believe that Hitler was an evil man or not?'

'Of course he was.'

'Right, I think most people would say the same thing. Now, if someone did not believe there was such a thing as right or wrong, then he or she could not accuse Hitler of doing wrong by exterminating six million Jews during the Second World War. The fact is that what Hitler did was not only wrong, it was downright evil with a capital 'E'. Go to Auschwitz in Poland and, I assure you, you will be confronted with the reality of evil. But, then again, we're going back to this question of choice because, at some point, Hitler must have chosen to implement the final solution in full knowledge of what that would entail. He was an evil man because he chose evil. In short, you become what you choose.'

'But what's all that got to do with abortion?'

'Well, while Hitler was responsible for the death of six million Jews, we're responsible for the deaths of five or six million unborn children since 1967, when abortion was legalised. The only difference here is that the Holocaust is universally recognised as evil, while abortion isn't. Yet, what you are actually doing to an unborn child is taking away his or her own right to live. Nothing can justify that.'

'Hmm...'

'I mean,' I continued, 'Hitler was an evil man, but look all around you – there's evil everywhere – you only have to switch on the news to find that out, and what does it come down to? Human choice. That's why you can't blame God for social injustice, or any other kind of injustice for that matter, because He will always respect people's right to choose between right and wrong. The only point is, what goes round, comes round and, in the end, all those good and bad decisions that you have made during your whole lifetime will come back to you in one form or another. As far as I'm concerned, it's better to be a sheep rather than a goat because, at the end of it, you'll be happy, and that's not something being a goat will bring. Basically, a person determines his or her life by the decisions he or she makes, even though there are some things you cannot change.'

'For example?'

'For example, your parents. You've often heard it said that you can choose your friends, but you can't choose your family. That is so true. I suppose it's not a question of choosing your family but choosing how you relate to them that counts, because you can't always choose what happens to you, but you can choose how you react to what happens. Life is all choice, choice, choice. I mean, you're choosing to listen to me right now, and I'm choosing to speak to you. You just can't get away from choice. The thing is, if everybody did take it upon themselves to make the right choices, the world would be a different place, and it's not idealistic to say so.'

'What do you mean by "idealistic"?'

I explained.

'Anyway, coming back to what I was saying, the world would be a different place. There wouldn't be crime, poverty and injustice. There would be a completely different order to things, totally. There wouldn't be AIDS.'

'Why's that?'

'Because, if everyone chose to stay with one partner during their lifetime, there would be no sexually transmitted diseases. It is as simple as that. Then again, you've got to believe it is as simple as that, because you can also choose to believe what you want to believe, disregarding what's true or not. You know, people very often don't opt for the simple explanation of things because they consider it too easy. They believe that, somehow, life must be complicated but, in all fairness, the truth is often enough very simple; it simply requires a willingness to find it.'

'Hmm!' said Shameel, as though tasting a sugary substance for the first time.

'Things that make you go "hmm",' I said, quoting a song from my youth.

'You know,' she said, after a moment of silence, 'that was the mother of all philosophical cigarette breaks.'

'Well,' I responded, sensing our time was up, 'shall we choose to go back to work?'

'Let's,' sighed Shameel.

14

The Beautiful Game

A few years ago, after the turn of the millennium, a survey was carried out among devoted football fans to ascertain how much of their lives revolved around their favourite sport. The results showed that a large proportion of the devotees' conversation focused entirely on football while much of their lives meant following their teams to away matches and spending substantial amounts of money on transport and tickets in the process. The survey also pointed out that many fans suffered from depression at the end of the season due to their teams not playing.

I must say that, in my lifetime, I have only ever been to one professional football match, played between Stoke and Hull. There, I could clearly understand the exhilaration of the crowd watching their teams battling it out for victory on the pitch. However, I quickly realised that the topic of football did not strike a personal chord in my own field of interest and it was on the train from Stoke-on-Trent one Saturday evening a long time afterwards that I had difficulty extricating myself from a football fan obsessed with filling my head with his knowledge of the game. Needless to say that this person would have been an ideal candidate for the above-mentioned survey.

Sitting down near a window in an empty carriage, I began reading a book to fill the time it would take to go to Birmingham. Five minutes into the journey, there appeared a group of five Leicester City football fans rushing down the aisle, while collectively chanting the words 'Blue Army!' a dozen times before settling down in a row of seats further down the carriage. Their chant alternated between D and C sharp, before rising one octave to then return to the original notes. They began again to sing the words. I put the book away, fully aware that I would not be able to concentrate. The fans' talk was all about the disappointing score between Leicester City Football Club and Stoke and how their team was going to come back to make it 'all the way'. Very frequently, their speech was interspersed with the strongest offensive vocabulary, prompted by the fact that they were all under the influence of alcohol. Occasionally, they would burp loudly for the sake of it and amused themselves by crushing empty Boddington cans to then throw them all over the carriage. I considered changing carriage when, suddenly, one of them got up to go to the toilet. He walked past me, looked around and stopped to gaze intently upon my person. For a few seconds, his expression resembled someone who had been hit by a flashing bolt of enlightenment. He then opened his mouth and pronounced to me the following words: 'Mate, you look like the kind of guy who's crossed a vast ocean in the engine room of a steamboat. Everybody else gets the credit for doing it while you get nothing, even though you made the boat work!'

At this, I was lost for words.

'Sorry, mate,' he said, 'I always come out with things like that when I'm drunk. Did you hear about the match?'

'Kind of,' I answered.

'We lost, 3-1. Ah well, never mind. Hold on a sec, I'm just going to the toilet.'

I decided to stay seated, seeing that this man was unexpectedly polite.

He duly came out and sat next to me, while leaning over my arm-rest. He was a plump, dark-haired man with a huge bald patch, who seemed to be in his forties. He began by gauging my interest in football, before embarking on a full-blown twenty-five minute talk on the topic, despite my evident lack of enthusiasm,

'So, what team do you support?' he asked.

'None at all.'

'None at all?' he remarked, while raising his eyebrows. 'Where have you been hiding? In a cave, like? Ah well, whatever floats your boat, I suppose. Oh, I get it, you're the kind of person that supports your own legs, 'cos your own legs support you!'

He laughed at his own joke. Meanwhile, his mates at the other end began singing fresh chants of 'Blue Army!'

'So,' he continued, 'who's your favourite football player? I mean, if you had a hundred million pounds to spend as a football manager, who would you buy?'

'I don't know, I'm not into football.' I said, a little painfully.

'Have you ever heard of Keith Gillespie or Dion Dublin?'

'No.'

'They play for our team: the Foxes. Yeah, Keith Gillespie, right, is a midfielder and Dion Dublin is a forward. I tell ya, you see some crackin' goals, like, you know. We've also got James Snowcroft, who's a forward, Jordan Stewart, who plays in midfield, Chris Makin, who's a defender and Nikos Dabizas, who's also a defender.'

He waited a while for an answer.

'*And,*' he said, 'we've got Ian Walker as goalie, Peter Canero, who's a defender and Danny Tiatto, who's a defender as well. With all that, do you know anything about the England squad?'

'I'm afraid not.'

'Well, there, you've got David Beckham, who's captain, of course, and who plays for Real Madrid, Micheal Owen, who's a striker and also plays for Real Madrid, David James and Rio Ferdinand. Rio Ferdinand plays for Manchester United and so too do Gary Neville and Wayne Rooney but, guess what, they all play for England as well. Then you got Steven Gerrard, Frank Lampard and Ashley Cole, who play for other teams like Arsenal or Chelsea. So, out of all that, who would you choose?'

'Look, I'm really sorry, but I really haven't got a clue as to who most of these people are. I'm not interested in football and I don't know anything about it. I'm sorry.'

'Come down with us. Our next game's against Nottingham Forest at home. It'll be a laugh, like, you know. We don't go in for violence, we don't. Nah, we're the lads, like, you know, but we keep it at that. It's just that, at the end of the day, football is just a beautiful game.'

'Thanks for the offer, but as I said before, I'm not into football.'

He carried on talking for what seemed an age on how the Barclays Premiership used to be Division One and how Divisions Two, Three and Four respectively became the Coca-Cola Championship followed by Coca-Cola Leagues One and Two. I was puzzled even more by the scores of footballer's' names he used to display his profound knowledge. Apparently, my ignorance on the subject fuelled his desire to unload the wealth of information he possessed.

I grew tired.

'So,' he continued, 'who do you reckon will win the next World Cup in 2006?'

At this point, I wanted no more.

'I don't know,' I sighed. 'Japan?'

'Japan? You must be joking, mate. Nah, Germany -- I'll tell you why. In the past, only seven teams have won the World Cup. They are Uruguay, Argentina, Brazil, Germany, Italy, France and England in '66. Now, if you look at the statistics, right, every time the World Cup is played in Europe, a European team wins and every time it's played out of Europe, a South American team wins. The only exception to this rule was in 1958 when Brazil won in Sweden. Now, the next World Cup is in Germany, so, following these statistics, a European team should win. So that leaves us with England, France, Italy and Germany. France and England, right, I don't count, because they've only won the World Cup on home soil. So that leaves us with Italy and Germany. Personally, I'm going for Germany, although you can never write off the Brazilians. Then again, when the Germans play badly they still get to the final of the World Cup; just look at the last one! So just imagine how they'll play on home ground. Having said that, though, they did lose 5-1 to England in the last World Cup qualifiers, and that was played in Germany, so you never know, but in a certain way, I don't like the Germans, nor the French for that matter, so I won't mind if any of them lose. Still, we've got a French player in our side: Lilian Nalis.'

Finally, when I actually started taking an interest in his insight on World Cup statistics, he was called away by his mates who had begun wondering what he was up to.

'Blimey,' he finished, 'you really don't know much about football, do you?'

He walked off and began a new 'Blue Army!' chant.

I arrived in Birmingham and got off the train, recapping in my mind what it was like to be with someone who spoke only of football.

15

Child's Folly

In my opinion, there is no more accurate a saying than the one found in Proverbs 22:15, which reads: 'Folly is bound up in the heart of a child'. I say this on account of a dangerous experience I had in the French Alps at the age of eleven, which certainly proves the veracity of the verse. It must be remembered that, normally, children are not aware of the consequences of their actions, and this may contribute in a large part to the 'folly' spoken of. In any case, at eleven, it was certainly apparent with me.

I begin by recounting how my mother always used to spend the summer holidays driving around France, visiting almost every single church we came across. At eleven, the idea of constantly visiting churches does not strike a chord in the heart of a boy. Still, there was one particular place of worship that did strike a chord because of its mere location, and that location was the alpine shrine of Notre Dame de la Salette. To get there by car, one had to take a long, winding road in the mountains that climbed ever higher from the safety of the valley below. Occasionally, one would see a coach full of tourists slowly negotiating the hairpin bends that characterised the way upwards. Needless to say, it was a sight that always made your heart skip a beat considering the narrowness of the road and the fact that there were few barriers between the road and the steep green mountainsides. In short, the higher one went, the more one marvelled at one's progress, until finally, one reached the shrine. There, one finds is a church (surprise, surprise!) adjoining a pilgrims' complex, whose interior decor reminded me of that of an airport. We remained there for several days.

Soon, after growing bored with the same surroundings because, as a boy, 1 became easily bored, I asked my mother whether I could follow one of the footpaths leading away from the complex. She approved. I also thought it was a good way of getting a healthy tan, for it is quicker to tan at altitude than at sea level. I took off my T-shirt and began walking. The path I followed was more or less a horizontal one, taking me past herds of goats bleating away on high valleys interspersed below the higher, more challenging climbs. I walked for forty-five minutes or so and decided to head back the same way. I had a real sensation that everything around me was 'living art', from the sun in the sky to the sound of the bells around the goats' necks. The afternoon had given me a beautiful image of vitality, perfectly combined with the pure mountain air softly blowing through the blades of grass. The memory is a fond one. Yet, coming across a perfectly perched boulder on the outer edge of a mountain's footpath, I stopped to gaze at it, wondering why I had missed it on my way outwards. It was not very large, as far as boulders go, but you would most certainly not ignore it were it to go tumbling down a hill at speed. It would be enough to trigger loud alarm bells in your mind, especially if it was heading in your direction.

Without so much as giving it a thought, I booted it three times before it began rolling downward. There I was, watching it bounce and leap at speed, when suddenly, out of the corner of my eye, I saw a red car 250 metres further down to my left, leaving the shrine on its way back. I was immediately gripped with fear. Only then did I realise the direct consequence of my action. I looked at the rolling boulder and then at the trajectory of the approaching car: they were on a collision course. My timing could not have been better even had I tried to target the moving vehicle. I became a nervous wreck. I made as though to pull my hair out but then began rocking backwards and forwards in a crouched position with my hands clasped together. I looked like someone who had severe constipation and I began wailing. 'Shit! Shit! Shit! Shit! Shit!' I shouted through my tears. If anyone had seen me on the track, unaware of what had happened, they wouldn't have known whether to laugh or feel sorry for me. I remained in that posture for the next thirty seconds, hearing in my mind all the expressions of French fury unleashed on me and my mother after the accident. With all of my being, I wished I could reverse the situation and put an end to this terrible moment of desperation. Indeed, I was raw with painful anxiety.

Finally, after straightening up, I dared look down the mountainside to notice that both the car and the boulder were out of view. This was due to a big bulge in the mountainside that covered them from where I was standing. As a result, I had to wait a few seconds longer before the terrifying outcome was affirmed. If I did not see the car appear to the right at the bottom of the bulge, I was doomed.

The seconds of torment passed and ended with relief when I saw the car coming into view, apparently unharmed by any falling boulder. Without any further ado, I simply dried my tears, looked over my shoulder to ensure no-one had seen me and casually continued walking. Later, I came across a diverging path leading down from mine and running away from the shrine, thus running closer to the road. I concluded that the boulder must have been stopped in its tracks by the much larger width of this lower path, since once the boulder had landed, its motion was no longer fuelled by a steep incline.

I got back to the shrine and silently promised myself never to do that again.

16

The French Language

In France, 'pff...', expressing the indifferent state of mind of an individual, often prompts the thought that not only does he or she not care, but that he or she does not even mind not caring. Where else has the expression of not giving a hoot been so wonderfully captivated with the contraction of the lips accompanied by a blowing out of air than in France? This chapter, however, focuses on an issue that no Frenchman, young or old, should purse his lips to, particularly when dealing with a topic that means so much to French identity: the language.

The French language is often quoted as being the language of love. Whether this derives from its natural poetic quality or its deep nasal intonations, I do not know, but what I do know is that it is being assailed in such a way that every time I talk to a young French person, I am automatically disarmed in a linguistic sense by the amount of new English words he or she uses. In all respects, French is being assailed by the Anglo-Saxon tongue. On going to France, I am always happy to hear the very latest in Anglo-American pop entertainment. I do not complain because frequently, French taste in foreign music is very similar to my own. Everywhere from supermarkets to TV adverts, one can sing along to tunes such as 'Getaway' by Texas or 'Signs' by Snoop Dogg, featuring Justin Timberlake, not forgetting other melodies that display equally colourful rhythms. Yet, in the 1990s, Jacques Toubon, the French Minister of Culture, put forward a bill proposing, among other things, that at least 60 per cent of all songs aired by radio DJs be sung by French artists. This was to combat the seemingly ruthless infiltration of British and American pop tunes often heard on the lips of youngsters. It is in the comfort of French people's homes that their children listen to English-sung lyrics and have recourse to the nearest English-French dictionary to look up all the words they do not understand. Hence, the actual coining of Anglo-Saxon words into the French tongue.

In the same way that English, in its relatively undeveloped state, was besieged by a flood of French words up to 300 years after the Norman conquest in 1066, it is now France's turn to be on the receiving end of a linguistic invasion. This is further achieved by the international media, which acts as a vehicle for new foreign word imports. Seemingly gone are the days when the French language could nestle comfortably alongside the English one, keeping its distance from the latter, but knowing full well that it was a world-class language, being used in the spheres of diplomacy and commerce, secretly competing in a major battle against the English adversary. In have come the days when French has grown to realise the true domination that English has come to exercise, not only on the international pop scene, but in world affairs also. The French, by all standards, are concerned about it, or, at least, the older generation is. It is afraid that the younger generation do not understand the importance of culture-preservation, while fighting to keep everything pure in the language of Corneille. How their hearts must sink on hearing the likes of *le drink*, *le deal* and *le friend* used by teenagers who deem it cool to voice them. One could even compose whole sentences where the main French nouns have been replaced with their English equivalents: '*Ce weekend, je suis allé avec mon friend à un garden party*' ('Last weekend, I went with my friend to a garden party.').

Sometimes, an English word has been borrowed only for its original meaning to be changed and remoulded into a new one. 'Space' has lost its reference to an open area and, in modern-day colloquial French, has come to mean 'strange', even though the French have their own word, *étrange*. The English phrase 'time up' no longer signifies that one's time has run out, but has come to mean 'a timetable', even though the French have their own *horaire*. Other less intrusive linguistic phenomena include the tendency for the younger generation to cut off the endings of many common words. This can be found in the phrase: '*Cet aprèm, je vais à la fac, comme d'hab,*' otherwise formally rendered in in the textbooks as: '*Cet après-midi, je vais à la faculté, comme d'habitude*' ('This afternoon, I am going to the university faculty, as usual'). Again, it is deemed cool by most French students to talk in that way.

In a fashion, I do sympathise with elderly French people, who, for example, had witnessed the putting up of German signposts during the Second World War in Paris. For them, to daily put up with English words in conversation may remind them of the linguistic invasion they endured during the last great war. On reading this, many must think that French sensitivity to the utilisation of English words in their language has been overly dramatised. To bring the point home, may I invoke the name of someone who is barely known in the UK but who, across the English Channel, has incited the minds of many to regard the rapid American installation of its own culture (and inevitably its language) as an undisputed menace. José Bové, from Perpignan, was a well-known French activist fighting for the liberation of France from an unwelcome English and American influence. In 2001, he was arrested and tried for having burned down a McDonald's fast-food restaurant, which was in the process of being built. Far from stoically accepting the American-owned business venture in his homeland, he saw it necessary to champion a cause that too many young people are too lax to embrace. His burning down of a foreign-owned culinary establishment was more a statement than an act. Presumably, he could no longer tolerate the ensemble of Anglo-Saxon words, American food and other sorts of British and American enterprises, such as Virgin Megastores and Disneyland outside Paris, the former opening the gates to countless words and lyrics reflecting Anglo-American culture. His immediate response was to target the biggest and most widespread foreign enterprise of them all: McDonald's.

Somewhere, I was once told by a supposedly learned man that language and culture are one and the same. I have to disagree. Culture and language are not the same, although they can be said to be closely related. A perfect example of this is precisely what has been described above. In absolutely no circumstance do the French feel they are borrowing from us, the British. Rather, they are borrowing from the US, whose culture has seduced them by fast-action TV series, films and the aforementioned music. As one

Frenchman once said on television, 'The only time I think of England is when I see it from the plane on my way to the States.' Real English culture, therefore, is brushed aside. The English language, however, which historically made its way to the States, is brought back across the Atlantic to France, where, at the same time, small elements of American culture have tagged along. Otherwise, if English culture had not been sifted out on its transatlantic journey, the French would have readily adopted tea-drinking and cricket as a national pastime. As we know it, they have not, although, obviously, there are some who drink tea (but none who play cricket).

Besides, to affirm that culture and language are one and the same would be to admit that England, America, Australia, New Zealand and Canada all share the same culture, as would France, Belgium, Luxembourg and the whole of Quebec.

17

Intelligence

How would you cope if you were stuck in the Alaskan wilderness, with no-one to help you, armed with a penknife, and faced with a giant brown bear who was stalking you for his supper? This is the precise scenario played out in the 1997 film *The Edge*, starring Anthony Hopkins and Alec Baldwin, where a billionaire businessman and a photographer find themselves pitched in a battle for their own survival. Gone is the relative ease and comfort of modern-day Western living and in comes the time to draw on one's practical and tactical intelligence to tackle the bear. This may be easy enough to point out, but isn't it true that by coming from a society where most things are acquired with little effort, one is not always encouraged to develop an advanced state of practical or tactical intelligence? Luckily, the character played by Hopkins remembered enough material from an old survival book to kill the bear and then head for safety.

I mention these two forms of intelligence because in the above situation, they would be the most important capacities to have. What use would it be to speak fifteen languages or be able to solve complex mathematical problems when confronted with the live or die theme portrayed in the film? All that would be rendered unnecessary. Instead, one would have to return to the hunter-gatherer state of existence and depend entirely on one's ability to make use of the forest around one. For example, how would you go about making a shelter or a fire? How would you eat? These are the questions that would need to be addressed in quick fashion, and that is what *The Edge* brings out in dramatic style. There is no doubt that the few remaining Native Americans in that part of the world would have a lot to teach us.

So far, several types of intelligence have been touched on. They are practical, tactical, linguistic and numerical intelligence.

Therefore, when talking about such a topic, one realises that intelligence comes in many different forms. If we were to extend this list, one could add musical, organisational and strategic intelligence, as well as many others. The last one must have been the kind of intelligence Napoleon had in abundance since all too often he won on the battlefield. It is also the same kind of intelligence a professional chess player has. Mozart obviously had a very developed musical intelligence that allowed him to wonderfully put together the richest of sounds, while Einstein had an enormous science related intelligence, which enabled him to unlock the secrets of the universe. Here, I am using famous figures who perfectly illustrate the varied nature of intelligence but who, at the same time, show how we are all intelligent in a greater or smaller capacity. Needless to say, most of us fit the second description.

Still, one can easily identify the kind of intelligence another has by whether he or she is more inclined towards the sciences or the arts. I think it is fair to say that nearly all of us fall into one or the other. If one leans more towards the sciences, one is more likely to have a greater understanding of numbers and equations, while those who lean towards the arts will have a clearer understanding of music, literature and graphics. It follows that the mental disposition of the mind to arts or sciences will push a person into one of the two directions. Yet, how does one account for those individuals whose minds cope just as well in both fields? This was found in remarkable fashion in the person of Leonardo da Vinci, who managed to combine his artistic talents with special scientific innovation to produce sketches of submarines or helicopters centuries before they came into being. I suppose one concludes that such a disposition comes more rarely and the genius of da Vinci more rarely still.

Indeed, today, specially designed tests are often used to measure a person's intelligence by gauging their capacity on various levels of understanding. For example, in an IQ test, one will have to resort, among other things, to one's linguistic and numerical skills to perform well. Afterwards, the points are tallied up and one will have a general idea of one's own intelligence. Yet it is true that some people work well in pressurised conditions, while others do not, since it must not be forgotten that these tests have a certain time allotted to each question. If I were to give you the sum '896 divided by 4' to work out in seven seconds, surely the time factor would push you up a gear to reach your answer. For those of you who have worked out the answer in the allotted time, good. For those of you who have not, it may simply be that this method impedes your ability to flourish properly. Hence, it may be argued that a person may be bright, while failing to perform in the wrong type of environment. Besides, revealing your IQ can sometimes invite others to alter their perception of you, which, in the end, may not necessarily be accurate. For instance, having a high IQ may breed hidden jealousy in your best friend, while having a below-average IQ may urge people to treat you with silent contempt. Then again, all this depends entirely on how much importance one attributes to intelligence.

It was while I was a schoolboy that I had my first experience of such a test. It focused on mathematics and it was with flushed cheeks that I entered the classroom, after arriving five minutes late. While everyone else had started, I had been busy racing down corridors to get there. I sat down and quickly opened the front page to answer as best as I could. Around me, I noticed the brighter members of the class put pen to paper in eager anticipation of what their final result would be. By all appearances, this was a chance to let one's intelligence shine. Forty minutes later, we handed in our papers to the teacher, who seemed bemused at the fact that I had only reached half-way through the test. My classmates then began speculating on their performance and could hardly contain themselves until the next morning, when their marks were to be disclosed.

As it happened, my mark came out as 'minus twelve'. Whether this meant my mathematical intelligence was twelve points below the national average, or that I had a negative IQ I do not know, for it was never explained, but understandably, it did nothing to flatter my self-esteem. To have the result called aloud in class was about as embarrassing as having one's trunks pulled off while diving in a swimming pool under the gaze of spectators. My classmates looked at me with wide-eyed astonishment, holding back any comment lest it cause offence. It was natural to know what they were thinking.

Mercifully, another girl had achieved a minus score, though none were surprised. As a result, that particular morning does not hold for me the fondest of memories, even though there was a specific reason why I had fared badly. The previous day, in my rush to catch up on lost time, I had failed to read the front page instructions, which stated clearly that points would only be awarded for correctly answered questions, while points would be deducted for wrongly answered questions. Questions left unanswered would be left unmarked. In a certain sense, then, it would have been better not to answer at all since my result would have been twelve points higher. It was my mistake, therefore, to have lost time and points on the more difficult questions I was under no obligation to answer, although innocently unaware of the test's real format. Besides, how can anyone have a negative IQ? That would be like putting someone's intelligence on a par with that of a bear or gorilla.

Several years later, I took another IQ test, a more conventional one this time and under more relaxed conditions to put my mind at rest. Without actually revealing the result, let us just say that it helped to erase that embarrassing moment at school.

Finally, while talking about such a topic among a group of friends at a restaurant one evening, I noticed that it was not always intelligence that was at the forefront of every individual's thoughts. We spoke about intelligence tests and argued briefly on who had the greatest IQ.

'Yeah, well, I believe I would have the highest IQ but would not do so well in a general knowledge test.' said one.

'And I believe that I would do pretty well in a general knowledge test but wouldn't be so good on the language side of things in an IQ test,' said another.

Meanwhile, one member of the party who, up to then had been quiet, spoke up for the first time.

'Anyway, it's not what you've got up there,' he said, gently tapping his temples, 'it's what you've got there.'

He pointed to his heart.

We remained silent for a while until another more talkative chap opened his mouth to say the following: 'Yeah, yeah, I see your point, but what I always heard is that it doesn't matter what you've got up there in your head or there in your chest, but what counts most is what you've got down there.'

He was pointing at his crotch.

We all laughed but then concluded that, disregarding the last point, it was not the kind of intelligence you have, but what you do with it that is most important of all.

18

A Study in Wealth

If a genie were to suddenly appear before you and offer you the choice of either leading a super-rich life or an incredibly poor one, which one would you go for? I think it is fair to say that most of us would choose the former. Today, we live in an age of 'free money', where such a fantastic scenario is not so far removed from reality. Switch on the television and you will see the likes of *Who Wants to Be a Millionaire?*, *The Vault* and *The Big Call*, not forgetting the number of scratch cards and other money-winning schemes that could all theoretically change one's life in an instant. It is almost an inevitable admission to say that we know at least one person who has taken part in these prize-giving competitions. Yet, can one be so categorical as to affirm that money buys you happiness? That is the eternal question that one has to think about before answering.

I, for my part, would like to examine a particular episode of my boyhood holidays in Paris to fully bring out the essence of living in dire financial straits. I begin with the memory of an early morning rush hour in the Parisian Metro. There, amid the chaos and pushing of commuters cramming in to fill up every available space on an underground carriage, I noticed that, for some reason, a circle with a radius of one and a half metres had opened up around an elderly man who was chewing the end of an empty pipe and who had a large bulbous nose covered in blackheads. It must be stated that there was no-one in this circle except for the elderly man in the middle. Being a young boy of eight, I was driven by curiosity to find out why this beggar was being singled out. I momentarily left the hand of my elder relative to push through the crowds and enter the spacious circle. At first, I was content at the thought that I had managed to find a place where I could breathe more easily. I could not have been more mistaken because what came next was the most vicious stench that had ever assailed my young nostrils. It is no exaggeration to point out that the beggar had probably not changed out of his garments for the previous four to five years. The odour hit me in much the same way as with smelling salts, causing me to reel back at its ferocity. I immediately rejoined the crowd of commuters and went back to my relative. Otherwise, everyone just stood in grim silence.

This may have been an extreme case of poverty but it only takes a book like George Orwell's *Down and Out in Paris and London* to understand the feeling of complete deprivation that may befall the unfortunate homeless person. There are varying levels to being poor but if we are to take the dictionary definition and apply the state of having to do without adequate food, clothing and warmth to ourselves, then it is only logical to think that money will, in some ways, make you happier.

However, I believe this is true only insofar as having enough cash to cover one's material needs, for anything exceeding that may lead to hardship of a different kind altogether. I say this in light of a recent visit to a special home catering for those with background difficulties. On being shown around the home, I was duly informed by a carer what category of people lived there.

'You might think,' he said quietly, 'that our residents come from very underpriviledged backgrounds, but in most cases, they come from very wealthy ones. They had absolutely everything that money could buy, but there was one thing missing, which they weren't given, and that most of us take for granted. That thing was l - o - v - e, love.'

These phrases made me ponder a while on whether it was money that made the world go round or the word just spelled out by the carer.

On the other hand, I have often heard it said that 'those who say that money can't buy you happiness are those who haven't got any money in the first place'. The verity of this statement would depend entirely on the individual attachment to money a particular person may have. For example, if you are not attached to a certain object, you will not mind keeping it or losing it, whereas, if you are, then you will do everything within your power to hold on to it. In a similar fashion, one could draw a ready comparison with the subject of wealth. Still, it is important to have reached the word 'attachment' because it is there that one finds the reason behind many people's pursuit of riches.

We have already seen one case of unhappiness linked to wealth but it would be interesting to ask what happens to the man who sets his mind on becoming rich, but who fails to fulfil his ambition in life. The answer is quite simple: he will become embittered. As a result of pinning his hopes on opulence, he will inevitably fall into the trap of coveting other people's riches and personally come out worse off. One could even put it down to his attachment to money.

Therefore, a little thought would have to be given before answering the genie, however extreme his offer may be. But that is the summary of this study; that wealth, in extreme quantities, or in sheer insufficiency, can lead to severe hardship, whether personal or material. We all need money: it is a fact of life. How would we cope without the little luxuries it affords us, whether they be cigarettes, chocolate or the odd pint, let alone the question of paying the bills, rent or mortgage? Then again, the point to grasp is how we relate to it. Do we really believe that wads of bank notes will personally make us better people? I do not know. But if there is one thing I do know, it is that being neither rich nor poor goes a long way towards finding a happy medium.

19

Providence

In Ireland, there was once a very poor young woman by the name of Rene, who had no money left to feed her two children. Not knowing what to do, she went out the front door and began walking aimlessly outside. In such a desperate situation, there was only one thing she could do, and that was to say the following words out loud: 'Oh God, I have nothing, nothing, not even enough money to get a loaf of bread for the kids.' She carried on walking in solitary silence. Suddenly, a gust of wind picked up and something landed on her forehead. She lifted her hand to pick it off and, surprise, surprise, it was an Irish one pound note. The wind carried on blowing and something else landed on her forehead. It was another one pound note. She pulled it off. She now had two pounds in her hands. Not believing her luck, Rene continued walking but then felt something else land on her forehead. It was another one pound note. At this moment, the woman in question had more than enough money to feed her children, considering how the episode took place in the 1960s. Obviously, someone, somewhere, had heard her.

This story was voiced to me seventeen years ago by Rene herself, who, by that time, was living in England and enjoying the company of her young grandchildren. Recently, she passed away, leaving me with an account that bears perfect witness to the extraordinary nature of providence.

Without knowing it until now, this story has most certainly shaped my perception of how, even in times of trouble, help is always at hand when all else fails. To be able to explain the dynamics of providence is nigh impossible, for one could spend an entire lifetime trying to figure out how it works without getting any closer to the answer, but one can affirm that it often swings into action when there is nothing humanly possible to do in severe strife. It was certainly the case with Rene, and it was while talking on the subject of providence with a certain gentleman that I became the victim of the most gross misunderstanding by someone who should have known better than to insult a fellow parishioner with a deeply callous selection of words. After all, here was a man who I know spends long periods of time in meditative thought, trying to engage his mind on relevant issues that one finds, very often, on the news. Unfortunately, however, his active thought patterns could not reciprocate the most basic analogy I was trying to convey in his living-room. We began our discussion on the subject.

'Well, basically, if you wanted to,' I said, 'you could live every day according to God's providence, from how you regard coincidental meetings in the street at home and abroad to how you view the money you need to pay the bills. I mean, in a fashion, it's a bit like one of those toys they released in the 1980s, where you have a kind of roadless bridge with which the child has to sequentially piece together the road from one end of the bridge to the other, while simultaneously setting off a slow-moving toy car that would inevitably fall off if one of the pieces wasn't fitted in time. I forget the name of it, but it was a good toy. You see, we are like the toy car that has to cross the bridge and, sometimes, you can't see the way forward because the road isn't pieced together. Yet, you've got to go forward, trusting that God will put the pieces together in good time. In short, you've got to trust that God will give you secure footing, although, sometimes, it's not easy to see. That, for me, is providence, in that, you might not see where your next pay cheque is coming from, or how you're going to live for the next week, but trust in God, and he will provide for you.'

'Yes, but you see,' said the gentleman, 'it's all very nice to believe in providence on a day to day basis, but that's not where the emphasis lies. You see, you can't spend your whole life believing that God will help you if you just sit around all day doing nothing.'

This was the beginning of the miscomprehension.

'Yes,' I answered, 'but who said anything about sitting around all day? That's not what I mean. I mean, there's an expression in France that conveys what you've just said, and that is, '*Aide-toi, et Le Ciel t'aidera'*, in other words, 'God helps those who help themselves'. And that is so true, because, if we were all sitting down on our derrières all day hoping that God would help us, then nothing would be done. Besides, that would be sheer laziness. No, that's not what I'm saying. What I am saying is that you do your utmost to provide for yourself and others but, when that fails, you simply have to rely on God to provide for you, because, firstly, there's nothing else you can do and, secondly, you can't do better than your best – it's impossible. In short, you do your best, and God does the rest. I mean, it's not rocket science written in Roman numerals, it's very simple.'

By this time, the gentleman had got completely the wrong end of the stick, which I had great difficulty taking in, considering the words he was about to use.

'Yes,' he said, rather cynically, 'but I think you're going down the Islamic path of things and basing your views on fatalism. I mean, what you're saying is a bit like a suicide bomber who says to himself, "Well, I'll leave it up to God's providence to decide who lives and who dies when I blow myself up." Surely, that can't be a good thing, can it?'

At this, my ears pricked upwards in much the same way as the ears of a dog do when surprised. If I had been obliged, on the spot, to give the gentleman marks out of ten for his gifted misinterpretation, I would have gladly given him full marks. This was a class A misunderstanding. I remained silent, not knowing how even to begin to disengage such a misconception from his mind. Sometimes, it is better to say nothing more, since, to do so would only antagonise the situation and, apart from metaphorically banging my head against the brick wall of miscomprehension, I did not want to have an argument in his own home. Still, it must be said that the fatalistic view that events are predetermined was very far from my mind at the time, for I am of the opinion that nothing is predetermined.

The gentleman went elsewhere and in the corner of the living-room was one of his children, watching the BBC news coverage of the famine in Niger. Having picked up on the word 'providence' and understood it, the boy asked me why it was that God did not provide for the thousands who were dying on the African continent. I looked at the TV screen, painfully watching a young baby gasping for air with infected lungs while in the throes of severe starvation. He was panting in such a way that indicated imminent death and, needless to say, it was a sight that made one's heart bleed.

'I don't know,' I answered. 'Maybe God is waiting to see if the rich and powerful come to their rescue.'

Meanwhile, I reflected on how the gentleman, the father of a number of children, could not understand the term 'providence' in its purest form. To explain its essence takes no more than a few words. In short, if we are to regard God as an all-loving father, then he will simply provide his children with what they need. It is as simple as that. All one has to do is believe it and the rest will work itself out.

Curiously enough, I finish with the last words spoken to me by Rene with both of us on a passing visit at the gentleman's house before her death. For some reason, while I was sitting next to her, she looked at me and said, 'You know, Christophe, you're not a believer of much, are you?' Again, I was at a loss as to what to say. It is strange to think that if there was only one thing I ever believed in, it was the providence God bestowed upon her way back in 1960s Ireland, when she had nothing left to eat.

20

A Conversation on War

Speaking to people is an essential part of travelling abroad. Firstly, if you spoke to no-one, you would soon become bored and, secondly, the things people say may be very interesting. For these two reasons, therefore, does dialogue constitute a major part in any travelling experience. Needless to say then, that in order to spark up a conversation, you often have to take the first step. This can be very rewarding in that, if you chance upon an 'open' person who also recognises the need for conversation, albeit with a total stranger, your previous feeling of boredom automatically disappears and, after a while, you are ready to continue on your journey. However, if you stumble across a 'closed' person, your attempts at making dialogue immediately make you wish you had never opened your mouth. This can happen a lot, although there is no way of quantifying how many people are 'closed' or how many are 'open'. Sometimes, you will be given the brush-off, and sometimes you will be accepted; there is no rule. Considering all these points, any time is a good time to initiate a conversation, and any place will do. The only thing to remember is that, sooner or later, your time with the interlocutor will come to an end and your paths will separate, with each party becoming personally richer with the new and individual viewpoint of the other. Encounters may be brief, lasting two minutes to two hours, but in the end, you are always satisfied at having warmed to the company of a fellow human being, regardless of creed, colour or sex.

In this spirit, and on the way to Paris by plane, did I meet a young and 'open' fellow traveller by the name of Vance, who was sitting near me towards the back. He was an American studying History at Nottingham University and was giving me his views on the War on Terror in such a way that I felt obliged to voice my own thoughts on the matter. We spoke freely and openly, seeing that the back of the plane was almost empty.

'Yeah,' he began, 'we had to go in there.'

'Iraq, you mean?' I clarified.

'Oh yeah, definitely. Do you know much about the Second World War?'

'A little bit.'

'Yeah, well, let me tell you, that the only reason the Second World War started was because we didn't do anything about Hitler in the first place. I just read a book about it and it says that when Hitler remilitarised the Rhineland in 1936, which he had absolutely no right to do, no-one took any action. If France or England had acted on that and gone straight in there, there might never have been a Second World War, because by then, we would've stripped Hitler of his power. But no-one did nothing about it. That's why, once he seized the Rhineland, he took it as an excuse to go ahead and build his army, which then led to the outbreak of war in 1939. In the same way, we just got rid of Saddam before he got too powerful. You see what I mean?'

'Yeah,' I answered, 'I see what you mean, but drawing that parallel is based on the premise that Saddam Hussein was indeed a global threat, which, personally, I don't think he was.'

'Hey, says who?' he laughed. 'Of course he was a global threat. Everyone knows that. It was only a matter of time before he acquired missiles of mass destruction.'

'Yeah, but don't you think that before the war in Iraq, the UN weapons inspectors were doing their best to determine whether he had any? Shouldn't they have decided whether he was a menace or not?'

'Huh, that was of no consequence. The point is that we're the number one country in the world. We're the only superpower. It's in our own interest and in everyone else's interest to ensure that we make this world of ours safe. It's not up to some country like Chile or Paraguay to do it – it's up to us. I mean, you can look at the long list of countries that have nuclear weapons – the States, Russia, China, France, Britain, Israel, North Korea, Pakistan and India. Man, we sure don't want to add Iraq to that list as well, do we? No, it's up to us.'

I refrained from answering, choosing to scratch an itch on my eyebrow.

'So,' he said confidently, 'this conversation getting to you?'

'No, no, not at all.' I said, seeing that he misinterpreted my scratching as a sign of insecurity on the subject.

'Yep, that's what it's all about,' he continued, 'learning from our past. You know, there's a theory of history that says that history tends to be cyclical, in other words, that history repeats itself, and that the only way of breaking free from this repetition is to learn from your past. And that's all we're doing.'

'Okay,' I admitted, 'you're the number-one superpower, and that's your so-called right, but with power comes responsibility. I mean, I understood the war in Afganistan because, obviously, the country was full of terrorist training camps and the like, but Iraq – I just don't see the connection.'

'I have to say this to many people, and I'll say it again here: there are many things we'll never know about. But I'm pretty sure we took the right decision.'

The conversation went silent for a while. I was taking aboard the scenery from outside while Vance just looked blankly in front of him. After a few minutes, I spoke up again.

'No, I just thought there were other options, that's all.'

'Oh yeah, and what would they be, bud?'

'Well, dialogue, for one. I mean, everyone knows the wickedness of 9/11, everyone, but the point is to ask oneself why such an atrocity was committed, even though it had no moral justification. All I know is that such acts are fuelled by the deepest of hates and, in order to tackle the problem, you have to understand what is causing the hatred. I mean, does the Arab world feel their people are oppressed by the States? Do they feel unjustly treated? Is it a historical problem? Do they feel misunderstood? I mean, there could be many reasons as to why they hate us, but with the use of dialogue and, possibly, the use of a third party, you just have to go to the root cause of things and ask "Why?".'

'Hmm, you can't negotiate with terrorists.'

'No, but bullets and war won't always solve your problems. And apart from that, there remains the question of how an Islamic country like Iraq will receive a Western model of secular democracy, bearing in mind how, in Muslim countries, religion and politics go together hand in hand.'

For some reason, Vance seemed slightly miffed at this and replied to the contrary.

'Whoever said that was true?'

'Well, it appeared to be the case with what I saw in Istanbul. Have you ever been to a Muslim country?'

'No.'

'Well, there you are. If you went to one, you would see what I mean.'

I based this last statement on an experience I had in a certain quarter of Istanbul several years ago, where I was curious to find out why a whole crowd of photographers and news reporters had gathered outside a large mosque. Also among the crowd were Turkish bystanders, eagerly expecting something. I waited among them, asking myself what the outcome of the event would be. After a few minutes, an enormous flurry of excitement broke out amid applause and flash photography as members of the government exited the mosque one by one to head back to their offices in their chauffeur-driven cars. People were jubilant and indeed, for them, the occasion was very important in that it demonstrated their leaders' testimony to the Islamic faith. This was something unseen in Europe, where no-one would ever applaud a politician for going to church. Therefore, outside the mosque in Istanbul, it struck me how politics and religion were heavily intertwined, not only in Turkey, but in other Muslim countries also. This is what Vance failed to recognise; that trying to implant a secularist-based rule in Iraq might be very difficult, considering how close the ties are between temporal and religious matters in their society. Still, it remains to be seen how this problem will be resolved.[*]

'Anyway,' coughed Vance, changing the subject, 'do you know Paris?'

---

[*] This conversation took place in April 2005. Since then, it has become widely acknowledged in many quarters that the War in Iraq has turned into a foreign policy disaster, with many in Iraq fleeing their country to escape the never-ending circle of violence.

With this, our conversation on the War on Terror drew to a close. Later, we touched on other topics of a less controversial nature. It is this kind of encounter that one finds effective at relieving the boredom on long or short journeys. Altogether, it was a helpful experience in that it enabled me to visualise the historical 'logic' of Vance's nation taking up arms far away. We arrived in Paris, and Vance and I went our separate ways.